CATAQUERIA ISLAND

Tabatha Taylor

Published by Anna Taylor
Publishing partner: Paragon Publishing, Rothersthorpe
First published 2020
© Anna Taylor 2020

Cover design: Gabhor Utomo

ISBN 978-1-78222-757-1

Book design, layout and production management by Into Print
www.intoprint.net
+44 (0)1604 832149

For my kittens!
Aaron, Harvey and Nicholas.

Contents

PREFACE

The sun shone brightly down on Pillow, heating him from his head to his toes. He purred with contentment at the warmth, and at the day's events. Excitement was in the air on Cataqueria Island.

Mickey had finally managed to convince Suzy Wong that he was a worthy husband. Now, their wedding at Willows Rock was only two weeks away. There would be a great feast of roasted mice marinated in ray fish oil, and lots of coconut milk with a touch of fermented sugar cane to put a swish in everyone's tail. Scratch and Socks had been instructed to find as many plump mice as possible, while Loops and Suzy Wing, who was Suzy Wong's twin sister, were to catch the ray fish for the wedding dishes. Twinkles was already practicing wedding songs to the delight of everyone but Tibby, who had run off to Mellows Wood to escape all the noise and commotion. He didn't care much for celebrations, especially weddings. And at the ripe old age of twelve, Tibby had given up on meeting a suitable mate of any sort, particularly given the pickings on Cataqueria Island.

Pillow looked up and smiled. Musette was coming toward him. When she reached Pillow, she swished her tail once and settled snugly in beside him. As they proudly soaked in all the excitement, they remembered their very first days on Cataqueria Island. A tiny dot in the central Pacific Ocean, the tropical island was only 33 miles long and barely 500 square miles in size. Thanks to its hot, humid climate, Cataqueria Island was lush and green. Its big lagoons swam with fish, and little pigs and fowl ran freely everywhere. Coconuts, bananas, yams, sugarcane, and exotic flowers grew wild. Mountain streams provided abundant fresh water for all the Cataquerians and the Doggeroes.

Yes, Cataqueria Island was a far cry from the world Pillow, Musette, and Tibby had grown up in, for they had come from England, where life had been very different indeed.

MR. & MRS. SUPREME

It all began when Musette and Pillow's owners, Mr. and Mrs. Supreme, had to relocate to Hong Kong. Mr. Supreme was a financial advisor, and the company he worked for was expanding. According to the world of finance, Hong Kong was the place to be, so that is where Mr. Supreme was to go.

Mrs. Supreme had always loved her cats and she was not going to leave them behind. Mr. Supreme, however, insisted she find good homes for them. He was worried about the cost of shipping two cats abroad. On top of that, he believed that adding two cats to the whole moving situation would only cause him and Mrs. Supreme even more stress. This major change in their lives was stressful enough.

But Mrs. Supreme had firmly put her foot down and refused to leave her dear friends behind.

Musette and Pillow had grown to love Mrs. Supreme. Since they were tiny kittens, they had loved spending endless hours cuddling on her favorite chair, squeezed tightly together like two little furry peas in a soft, safe pod.

Musette was just four weeks old when she moved in with the Supremes, at which time Pillow was almost a year old, so in cat years, he was a grown-up. At first, he'd been a bit resentful of Musette, who had stumbled and tumbled all over him, pulled at his ears, and flew headfirst into his dinner bowl. But by her second month in the household, Pillow could not help but notice how pretty and dainty Musette was becoming. Slowly but gradually, the annoying, podgy little kitten faded away, and a beautiful, slender, dainty cat, with copper-colored streaks in her sleek black fur, appeared. She had golden paws and a yellow streak running from the tip of her head to the end of her black, shiny nose. Her whiskers were evenly formed and her eyes sparkled like emeralds. She moved gracefully around the house, as if dancing to music.

Pillow was strong, firm, and jet black, with a white streak running from his head to the bridge of his nose. His eyes were as dark as the night sky, but often flickered with gold. He was sincere, able, and kind. And as Musette grew and matured, he knew he wanted her to be his mate.

One day when Musette was six months old, she and Pillow were cuddling together under Mrs. Supreme's legs. Musette, nestling into the silky black fur of Pillow's neck, felt there was nowhere in the whole world she would rather be.

"Musette, I know you're still only a kitten, but in January, when you turn eight months old, will you be my Cattona?" Pillows asked.

Musette began purring so loudly that Mrs. Supreme leaned down to stroke her. "Ah, listen to that happy little engine," she said.

"Hmm," replied Mr. Supreme with little interest. "Bloody cats," he muttered.

Musette giggled lovingly at Pillow's face. "Oh Pillow, I will! I will be your Cattona forever."

"And I will be your Catton forever, and will love and protect you until the day I die."

CROSSING PAWS

Pillow and Musette married that January at the end of the Supremes' garden. It was a small gathering with just close friends from the neighborhood. After the crossing paws ceremony, which took place under the apple tree, everyone feasted on prawns and fish brought by Mario, whose owner ran the local Italian restaurant, cat biscuits collected from various homes, and enough milk to fill everyone up. Musette looked beautiful and wore a tiara made of daisies with red cherries woven into the green stems of the flowers. Pillow was the proudest cat in the whole neighborhood.

During the next six months, the newlyweds spent their time stalking around the large garden, climbing trees, chasing butterflies, and being very much in love.

Right next door to the Supremes lived Tibby, a big, fat tabby cat with a round face. Lines of black fur perfectly encircled his head, setting off his grey base coat. His eyes were small, and his ears were pointed. He would often make Musette feel timid and frightened, which annoyed Pillow.

Sometimes when Tibby sat on the large wooden fence, Pillow would bite him on his fat rump, startling him so much that he flew into the blackberry bush in his garden. At that sound, his owner, old Mrs. Maple, would shuffle outside and bang on the fence with her stick to protect her Tibby. And, once again safe, he would wind himself around her legs, caressing them, as if to tell her how much he appreciated her looking out for him. But Musette and Pillow would leap through the cat flap on the Supremes' back door, run into the kitchen, scarper down the hall and rush into the living room, where they'd jump onto the sofa and roll around, laughing about Tibby.

Mrs. Supreme, hearing them and sensing their playful mood, would take a long velvet ribbon and dangle it before them. Pillow and Musette would chase, dive, and paw at the ribbon, learning how to be quick and agile. Thus, they became the best mice hunters in Beaconsfield.

Tibby, on the other hand, remained lazy, crafty, and sly. He was, however, extremely intelligent. He could open doors and cupboards, read newspapers, and had invented a kind of writing using the pads of his paws. He had discovered he could form messages by dipping a paw pad into mud, and then patting out the mud into patterns that meant different things. He began teaching all the cats in the neighborhood his paw-pad patterns and new language. Then he created a daily cat journal for Beaconsfield, leaving messages, news, and bits of gossip in all the local gardens.

For Pillow and Musette, life with the Supremes in Beaconsfield was very good until the evening Mr. Supreme arrived home looking rather irate and quite anxious. Musette and Pillow were both comfortably stretched out on the sofa. Before they could say "whiskers," an enormous row erupted between the Supremes.

"I don't want to live in Hong Kong! I love my home, my garden, my country, and all my friends! And what about the cats? I'm not leaving them, I just couldn't," said Mrs. Supreme.

"That's it, is it? It's those bloody cats! It's always them!" replied the very cross Mr. Supreme. "Do you know how much it will cost to ship those two moggies all the way there?!" he shouted from the top of his lungs.

Mrs. Supreme burst into tears and ran upstairs, sobbing into her hanky.

Mr. Supreme remained downstairs. He stared angrily at Musette and Pillow, muttering, "You won't be going anywhere other than to a cats' home, I promise you that!"

Musette huddled into Pillow, crying, "I'm so scared, Pillow. What is going to happen to us now?"

Pillow never said a word. He just stared back at Mr. Supreme without blinking once.

TWO BECOMES THREE

The following days in the Supremes' house were filled with tension and activity. No one even noticed Tibby sitting at the front door of Mrs. Maple's house day after day.

Then one evening, there was a loud knock at the Supremes' front door. Mrs. Supreme checked her face in the hall mirror, wiping away the mascara flaking down onto her cheeks, and fluffed her hair before heading for the door. Mr. Supreme followed her, wondering who could be visiting them at such an hour.

When Mrs. Supreme opened the door, both she and Mr. Supreme were surprised to find a policeman before them, looking quite serious. He was tall, broad, and pale, yet he had an air of kindness as he spoke.

"Good evening, sir, ma'am. I'm afraid I have some sad news regarding your neighbor, Mrs. Maple. We received a telephone call from the milkman who noticed that the milk bottles hadn't been taken inside her house for several days. Anyway, Mr. and Mrs.—?" The policeman paused, raising his eyebrows slightly.

Mr. Supreme held out his hand formally. "Supreme."

"Well, Mr. Supreme, as I was saying, you probably noticed the milk bottles accumulating next door, and I'm afraid it all leads to the obvious."

Mrs. Supreme gasped. *"Oh, no.* I hadn't noticed the bottles! You see, we have been having problems of our own!" And she burst out crying, for she knew what had happened next door.

"Now, now, Mrs. Supreme, she was an elderly lady and I believe her passing was all very natural."

Mr. Supreme put his arm around his wife's shoulders as she continued to sniffle.

The policeman continued. "Do you know if Mrs. Maple had any family or close friends we can contact?"

"I really don't know," said Mrs. Supreme. "I'd never seen her with anyone. She kept to herself, really. I believe she was a writer. All she had was that cat. I think his name is Tibby."

"Yes," said the policeman, "we found him sitting at the kitchen door meowing, clawing at the door, trying to get inside the house. Not our problem that one, I'm afraid. It's a shame, but I guess that's one for the cat protection team."

"Oh, no," Mrs. Supreme cried out. "The poor thing must be frantic!" She started to shove Mr. Supreme forward, pushing him out the door as she spoke. "Go on, dear, do go and get him. That's the least we can do."

Mr. Supreme, who didn't want to appear mean-spirited in front of the policeman, said, "Of course, dear. I will get him now."

Mrs. Supreme sighed and turned to the policeman. "Would you like a cup of tea?"

"No thank you, ma'am, although it is kind of you to offer. But I must dash. I need to get back to the station and write a report on Mrs. Maple. But I'm rather pleased to see her cat get a good home. It makes my job a little easier. Good night, and take care," he said with a kind smile. And off he went, turning once to wave at Mrs. Supreme.

Five minutes later, Mr. Supreme came back through the kitchen door carrying Tibby in his arms, which now ached a little. "Dear lord, did you eat Mrs. Maple?" he muttered as he plunked Tibby down onto the kitchen floor.

Mrs. Supreme chose to ignore that comment. She instructed Mr. Supreme to close the door so that Tibby had time to relax before meeting Pillow and Musette.

The Supremes sat together in the kitchen, chatting quietly while watching Tibby as he sniffed about. Eventually he scooted under the kitchen breakfast bar and crouched there, looking quite nervous.

"It's such a shame I never really knew Mrs. Maple," said Mrs. Supreme. "I mean she just kept to herself."

"Yes, I know, darling. And I need to say something to you." Mr. Supreme took hold of Mrs. Supreme's hand. "I'm sorry about the cats. I know that they mean a lot to you. And when I found poor old Tibby sitting outside Mrs. Maple's door, looking so bedraggled and lost, I felt terrible. Right then I realized that I really couldn't stand the thought of Musette and Pillow hovering around someone else's garden or back door, looking lost and left behind. I have decided that all three cats will join us in Hong Kong I will get my secretary Martha to arrange everything first thing tomorrow morning."

"Oh, thank you darling, thank you!" Mrs. Supreme kissed Mr Supreme on the cheek and then she raced over to Tibby. She picked him up and gently put him on her lap. As she petted him, Tibby began to purr, and somewhere inside him, so did Mr. Supreme.

TEMPER TAILS

Pillow thought furiously as he paced. *That fat leech Tibby from next door living here! And even worse, moving away with us!?*

Musette skipped about nervously. "Oh Pillow, what if we have to share a container with him when we're moving?"

"I don't know," Pillow replied. "But you mustn't worry, Musette. Just leave it to me. He won't annoy you, I promise. He wouldn't dare."

"Is he still in the kitchen?" Musette asked. "Will they leave the door open for us, so that we can get some milk?"

"Musette, don't be so dramatic," Pillow said.

In the kitchen, Mrs. Supreme almost jumped. "Goodness, what's that?"

Tibby, who had flown off her lap, was back under the kitchen breakfast bar.

"It's the cats," replied Mr. Supreme. "They're fighting. They know who's here and I don't think they are going to be pleased with our new lodger. You know what cats are like with their territory and all of that feline stuff." He shrugged his shoulders. "But they will all just have to learn to get on with one another and be bloody grateful we are taking them full stop." He grunted and thought, *I don't know why I bother.*

Mrs. Supreme went straight into the living room. She was surprised to find Tibby and Musette huddled on the floor, their heads practically buried into their necks. She sat down, patted the cushions, and spoke kindly.

17

"Come up here on the couch, you two."

Musette jumped up daintily, falling softly into Mrs. Supreme's lap with complete submission. Pillow followed and sat at Mrs. Supreme's side.

"Now, listen. Poor Tibby has lost his owner who was like a mother to him. Imagine if that happened to you. Do be kind to him. And I know you will all get along eventually," Mrs. Supreme said as she stroked Pillow with one hand and Musette with the other.

That night Tibby slept upstairs with the Supremes, snug and warm at the end of their bed. Downstairs, Musette and Pillow, who had calmed down by now, chatted quietly while they preened their fur and purred out beautiful tunes of love.

"You know what, Musette," Pillow said, "Mrs. Supreme was right. It must be awful to lose the person you loved and depended on, and to suddenly be all alone. Let's just try and get on with Tibby. He must be having a terrible time and we should be a bit more understanding."

"I know," said Musette sheepishly, "we have been a little unkind. Let's be welcoming to Tibby in the morning and see what happens. I know how we would feel if anything happened to our family. It would be so terribly tragic."

BREAKFAST

Tibby nervously followed Mrs. Supreme downstairs, staying close to her ankles and wondering if he was going to be formally introduced to his new family. To his surprise, Pillow and Musette were calmly waiting under the kitchen table for their breakfast.

"Good morning," said Pillow brightly. "How was your first night here with our dear Supremes?"

"I slept perfectly well, dear fellow. Thank you. And may I say, Musette, you are looking rather fine this morning," Tibby said politely.

"Thank you, Tibby. I am so sorry to hear about Mrs. Maple. You must be very sad at your loss."

"Yes, I am, Musette. But I have been fortunate your lovely family has taken me in. I do hope we can all get along, as I overheard we are going to Hong Kong. Can you tell me more about that?" Tibby asked.

"Well, our family have to move there because of something to do with work, I guess. We will be moving to a ground floor apartment in some fancy area of Hong Kong, so it should all be tickety boo," Pillow informed.

"My, oh my," said Tibby, pondering as he spoke. "This is going to be some adventure and I can't wait."

"Do you really think so?" asked Musette, looking surprised.

"Oh yes, young lady, it will be a wonderful experience for us all. We will be so cultured when we come back. I could then write about my travels! It would be most informative for the young. Yes, I could be the Phileas Fogg of Beaconsfield."

"More like Fogg's balloon," said Pillow and all three of them started laughing, feeling a lot more comfortable with their new friendship.

Mrs. Supreme began to prepare breakfast. She dished up fresh creamy milk with lamb's liver, added some dried biscuits, and spooned that into three little bowls, which she then placed side by side on the floor.

The three cats leapt to their dishes and began eating without any fuss.

"Well, it seems Tibby's appetite hasn't been affected," Mr. Supreme told his wife. "He seems very at home now. Amazing what a bit of food does, isn't it, love? Do you think if we popped our clogs the cats would even notice we had gone?" *Probably not,* he thought to himself, *if they were fed!*

Mrs. Supreme just ignored him. She knew her husband didn't really understand the animal world, so she just let things be.

It was a pleasant day. All three cats exchanged stories of how they grew up with their humans. Tibby was very interesting and well mannered. Pillow and Musette liked his company and were glad he was coming away with them. He was so knowledgeable but not at all arrogant, and they felt they could trust him with their lives.

That evening the three cats sat in the sitting room waiting to hear the *tap tap tap* of bowls.

"Something smells good," said Tibby.

"Yes, it's roast chicken, our favorite," said Musette "Did Mrs. Maple cook chicken for you?"

"No, I am afraid not. She used to have her food delivered by a lady who just put it in the freezer. I only was ever fed from a tin, which is what I got used to. But I was still very happy with Mrs. Maple," Tibby said.

"Well, Tibby, you're in for a treat tonight. Let's see it as a kind of celebration, a moving-in dinner for you."

"Thank you, Pillow, that's most kind of you. I will be delighted to dine with you and your wife. And if you don't mind, I would like to go next door and spend some time in my garden to show my respect to my dear Mrs. Maples.

"We understand, Tibby," said Musette. "We won't disturb you at all.

SAYING GOOD-BYE

The days seemed to fly by the and whole house was buzzing with excitement and anticipation about the upcoming move to Hong Kong. The longest trip Pillow and Musette had ever taken was to Devon. Mrs. Supreme's sister was married to Mr. Twiddle who used to live right around the corner from the Supremes. One day when Mrs. Supreme's sister was visiting from London, she accidently reversed into Mr. Twiddle's car. Mr. Twiddle lost his car's rear lights and bumper, but he found his future wife. He and Mrs. Supreme's sister fell in love at first sight. After they were married, they moved to Devon.

Mr. and Mrs. Supreme would travel down to Devon once a year, taking Pillow and Musette with them. The cats always enjoyed this. They were kept in a caravan at the bottom of the garden because Mr. Twiddle was allergic to cats. Pillow and Musette didn't mind not being allowed into the Twiddles' cottage. The caravan had every modern convenience you could imagine. Besides that, Mrs. Twiddle was quite neurotic. Wearing a white paper suit with plastic gloves and a mask, she would come into the caravan every morning to clean out the cat tray. Mr. Supreme said he thought she wanted to find an alien in there. She retorted that given what she found in the cat tray, that was a possibility. But for Pillow and Musette, these were romantic weekends, and they had cherished them.

Now, Pillow, Musette, and Tibby spent time in the garden, talking with other neighborhood cats about their upcoming move, which, although exciting, was also beginning to make them rather anxious.

One day Pillow and Musette were sitting with some friends next to the small fishpond in the Supremes' garden. Coburn, whose shiny black fur sparkled in the warm sun, grinned. "My master said, 'Let's hope the Supremes' cats don't end up in some Chinese takeaway. That would cause quite a stir fry'!" Coburn laughed and laughed while rolling around on his back as the other cats sat giggling.

Musette frowned and nudged Pillow. She did not want to listen to any silly nonsense from this alley cat that, she was sure, did not know China from Chigwell.

"Come on, Pillow, let's go," she said with an annoyed swish of her tail.

"Oh, don't go!" pleaded Sassy. "Please stay, Musette. We ought to make the most of the time we have left together."

Sassy was Musette's best friend. She was a beautiful Persian cat with fur as soft and white as marshmallows. She lived around the corner in Rose Cottage with one of the wealthiest families in the neighborhood. She was as catty as a cat could be. Even so, Musette enjoyed the privileged lifestyle Sassy so often spoke about and which perfectly matched her sophisticated nature.

"Sassy, I really must get back now. I need to make sure Tibby is okay as he hasn't been out much lately. Pillow and I are a little worried about him."

"Oh Musette, how could you worry about Tibby? He certainly has landed on his feet moving in with your family. I bet he is so happy now he's probably glad old Mrs. Maple has gone," said Sassy with a mischievous grin on her face.

"Sassy, how could you say such a thing!?" And with that, Musette skipped off with her tail in the air, expecting Pillow to follow, and he did.

Sassy turned to Coburn, who was watching the fish ducking and diving under the rocks in the glistening pond. She could just about make out where each one was hiding as she peered through the holes of the net, which protected the fish from the hungry birds above.

She loved to eat fresh fish. Her owners had a wonderful fish tank displayed in their bathroom to create a calming effect. Once Sassy had fallen in while grabbing a little goldfish and then had to spend the entire day at the Posh Pet's salon while waiting for a wash and blow dry. Her owners decided to cover the tank as Sassy was very unkind to the eye when wet.

"When my owner's cousin came back from China, she had a bag that looked very much like Pillow. So, who knows, they may indeed eat cats in China. I certainly don't envy Musette and Pillow going near there," Sassy said, gazing at her beautiful reflection in the pond. "It's such a pity, isn't it, Coburn?" she added, with a sigh.

"I know, Sassy. I will also miss them both," Coburn said sincerely.

Sassy turned to Coburn. "I meant the net. I'm feeling rather peckish."

Later, as the day ended, Pillow, Musette, and Tibby were huddled snuggly together on the large sofa with Mrs. Supreme. She was ticking her to-do list. Mr. Supreme was reading out loud from his Chinese phrase book, trying out words in this new language, and looking completely confused. The cats watched him, thinking he had gone quite mad.

Mr. Supreme held a pair of long, plastic chopsticks in one hand and tried to pick up some pieces of fruit on a plate before him. But he only managed to send the fruit flying into the air, nearly hitting Pillow on the head.

"Arse so!" Mr. Supreme shouted, causing Mrs. Supreme to nearly jump out of her seat.

"Dear, would you please stop being so stupid and help me remember what has to be done instead of messing around and playing silly games."

"It's only a bit of fun, dear," Mr. Supreme replied and rolled his eyes.

"If you lift those eyes any higher, they'll end up in heaven," Mrs. Supreme warned.

Mr. Supreme got up and bowed slowly. "I vill bling your tea in a moment, my lady," he said in his best Chinese accent, which made Mrs. Supreme burst out laughing. Then, with his hands clasped together in the prayer position, Mr. Supreme waddled out of the room like a big duck.

"Oh, just get on with it, you silly old fool," Mrs. Supreme said, chuckling as Mr. Supreme disappeared into the kitchen. She smiled at her dear companions, stroking them all gently. "Oh, I don't know," she sighed. "I hope we are doing the right thing. Well, whatever happens, at least you are all coming with me and we will all be together."

In the kitchen, as the kettle boiled, Mr. Supreme stared out the window at his beautiful garden. The sky was turning from pale blue to a rusty pink, and the evening was milky and dusky. Everything was so very English. Deep in his heart, Mr. Supreme knew he was going to miss home.

BOXES AND A BASKET

The next day started quite early. The removal vans had arrived, and little by little, the furniture and packing boxes were disappearing out of the house.

All three cats had wisely been kept in the kitchen since the previous evening. They had also been given very little food since Mrs. Supreme feared they might suffer travel sickness.

Musette, Pillow, and Tibby all sat still, hardly moving or talking. They stared at the large wicker basket, which had been left on the kitchen worktop. They knew they would be traveling in it for the first leg of their journey.

"Can't we escape?" Musette fretted, her eyes wide with fear and her voice quivering like jelly on a plate.

"Could you really do that to Mr. and Mrs. Supreme who've been so kind, loving, and generous to us?" Pillow asked.

Musette lowered her head in shame. "No, I guess not. I really don't want to go, Pillow, but you're right. I couldn't leave the Supremes."

"What about you, Tibby?" Pillow asked. "Do you want to escape? There would be no shame in you jumping ship, if you will excuse the expression."

"How very thoughtful of you, dear fellow," Tibby replied. "But I want to go. I am an adventurer. I am looking forward to seeing the Great Wall of China and getting to know more about the history of such an amazing country."

"We are not going to China, Tibby," Musette exclaimed. "And I thought you knew everything!"

"My dear Musette, I am impressed with your knowledge of geography, but what I mean is, once I get my bearings, I will leave you two in peace for a while and do some traveling. After I see a bit of the world, I will return. And to answer your question, Pillow, I don't want to leave the Supremes. They are good people and I am far too well off with them. And more importantly, I have grown very fond of you and Musette, so I am staying. I embrace this opportunity with gusto."

The kitchen door opened and in came Mr. and Mrs. Supreme.

"Do you think they will be all right travelling in the same basket, dear?" she asked.

"Yes, yes, they will be fine. It's best they all stay together. It will be less stressful for them," Mr. Supreme reassured his wife but thought, *and it will be a lot less expensive for me.*

At 9 a.m. it was time to go. Mrs. Supreme checked the cupboards, fridge, oven one more time, making sure that everything was spic-and-span for the new tenants who were arriving at noon. She had left milk, tea, and sugar, for she knew there was nothing better than a cup of tea after a long journey. She also left a list of useful information, such as when the bins were collected and what time the local grocery store opened and closed.

She put the list under the plant she had bought and didn't dare think too much more, as time was getting on. She picked up three new red velvet collars, all engraved with the cats' names and new address, and gently placed them around each cat's neck. Then Mrs. Supreme checked all the rooms to make sure no lights were left on.

When she returned to the kitchen, she breathed deeply. "Okay, my babies," she said, and picked Musette up first. She gave her a big hug and a kiss and gently placed her into the brown wicker basket on the kitchen table. Next, she picked up Pillow. "Now you look after Musette, my little boy," she said, holding him close to her chest and stroking the side of his soft face. Tibby was trying to jump onto the kitchen table but he couldn't manage. Pillow smiled. "Don't worry, Tibby, she won't leave you behind," he said as Mrs. Supreme placed Pillow beside Musette.

"I'm not taking any chances," Tibby said, excited.

"Come on, then, Pudding," Mrs. Supreme said, as she picked up Tibby. "Oh, my lord, Mr. Supreme was right. You are rather, er, sturdy. In you go, then." And into the basket Tibby went.

"Well, here we are," said Pillow. "All together in our basket short of a picnic."

"The odd sandwich wouldn't go a miss," Tibby added, as Musette laughed.

Mr. Supreme came into the kitchen. "That's it, love. Everything's packed, sealed, and ready to be shipped, including those three moggies. Now, what more can I do, dear?" he asked, smiling at Mrs. Supreme.

"You can carry them out to the car while I lock up, okay?" she said brightly.

"Certainly, darling, but first come here."

"Why? What do you want?" Mrs. Supreme asked.

"I want a cuddle, that's all. I want a cuddle from my wonderful wife who means the world to me."

"Oh, you daft old fool! We have no time for that."

"Oh, we do," Mr. Supreme said, and held his wife for a few seconds.

Mrs. Supreme hugged Mr. Supreme back and, after a moment, said, "Right, that's it then. Enough of that carrying on, love. Let's go." She picked up her bag off the worktop as

Mr. Supreme picked up the big wicker basket and headed outside.

Mrs. Supreme looked around her kitchen until she heard Mr. Supreme shout out, "Okay, darling, is everything locked up?"

"Yes," she called back and then headed out, whispering, "See you again, home sweet home."

Outside, Mr. and Mrs. Supreme had a quick chat with the driver who would be delivering the cats to the dock. He was an Indian man with a kind, warm face. "I hope you have a pleasant stay in Hong Kong. It's very far to go for a takeaway!" he joked.

Mrs. Supreme laughed as Mr. Supreme said, "It's a long way, but change is good." Wanting to speed things up, he tried to usher Mrs. Supreme toward the taxi that was waiting for them. She, however, stood peering into the taxi's backseat where the cats' basket sat.

"Don't worry, I will get these little fellas to their destination safely," the driver said.

"Thank you," said Mrs. Supreme, as Mr. Supreme took her arm and led her toward their taxi. "See you soon!" she shouted to the cats. "Be good and don't get up to any mischief."

Mr. Supreme looked a little embarrassed. "Come along, dear. The driver will think you odd, making such a fuss."

"Well, I don't care what he thinks," she said.

"Don't worry!" the driver shouted back to Mrs. Supreme, thinking, *They must have more money than sense taking their cats to Hong Kong.* "I will take great care of them!" he added.

And as the taxi pulled away, the cats shared a look, knowing this was it—they were leaving, and their adventure was beginning.

"Goodbye," said Musette, waving at the house. "Goodbye,

dear house. May we one day be back inside our wonderful home."

"Oh, Musette," said Pillow, "wherever you are is my home, darling."

With that the taxi roared like a great beast, startling Musette so much that she curled into Pillow's soft fur. Tibby peered out of the basket, catching glimpses of country lanes, isolated cottages, and busy towns flying by. Although his throat felt lumpy and his stomach seemed to have sunk, he remained in good spirits. "Are you two okay?" he asked cheerfully, checking on Pillow and Musette.

"Yes, we are, Tibby," Pillow replied. "The journey will be the hardest part of this adventure, but I am sure once we are all in our new home, everything will be just as fine as it was in our home here. In fact, I think everything will be even better."

"Umm," said Tibby. "I'm starving. I do hope we get fed soon."

"Oh, for goodness sake," Musette laughed. "It will do you good not to eat so much for a change, Tibby."

"Just saying, that's all," Tibby said with a shrug, as Musette and Pillow smiled at him.

HONG KONG AWAITS

Time seemed to fly by as the steady hum of the taxi's engine lulled the cats to sleep, snug and warm in the lovely basket. They had no idea they were heading toward the wharf, while Mr. and Mrs. Supreme, in another car, were heading directly for the airport to catch their flight to Hong Kong.

Mr. Supreme had made plans with a good friend who happened to be the captain of a cargo ship. He had offered to board the cats in exchange for a stay at the Supremes' plush new garden apartment in Hong Kong on East Wan Chai, which was one of the finest locations on the island.

The Captain informed Mr. Supreme that the cats would be kept on deck in one of the large metal containers normally used to transport livestock and general goods. On this voyage, the cargo ship would be empty of animals, so Sammy would oversee the cats. Sammy was a young journalist who was going to Hong Kong to try to get work at a television news channel. Since he had little money, he had accepted the offer to work as the Captain's personal assistant during the voyage. Sammy also knew this would be a real adventure, perhaps the kind that would allow him to tell the people he hoped to interview with that he had ideas for news stories about life aboard a cargo ship.

Mrs. Supreme was a bit reluctant when Mr. Supreme first told her about the plan to have the cats transported on a cargo ship. She wanted them to be flown to Hong Kong as well. But as usual, she had to reach a compromise with her husband, who liked to penny pinch. When she learned that the cats would be well cared for, their traveling cage was spacious and large enough for much larger animals, and they would even have an outdoor area where they could run around and get plenty of fresh air, she felt better and decided this seemed the next best option to flying them to Hong Kong.

Also, the Captain had promised to keep an eye on his feline passengers and told Mr. Supreme he would perhaps bring them into his cabin on the odd day if he had a few hours to spare.

So, Pillow, Musette, and Tibby slumbered away, unaware just how big an adventure they were about to begin.

9

DOCKING CATS

The cargo ship was 1,100 feet long and looked like a huge floating city. It would be on the water for nearly three weeks, departing from Southampton, heading toward Morocco, across to the Suez Canal, on to Singapore, and then straight up to Hong Kong. The weather forecast for the journey promised calm seas and pleasant temperatures.

As the car delivering them arrived at the dock, all three cats woke. Tibby was full of excitement. "Oh, this is such an adventure! Do you know what the great Marco Polo said?"

"No, what did he say?" Pillow asked.

"The man who goes to sea is a man in despair."

"And how is that going to boost our morale, Captain Positive?"

"Take no notice, Pillow," Musette suggested, swishing her tail.

"What I meant was, it's hardly the QE2, is it? I mean, really, we are not cattle!" Tibby huffed.

"Stop complaining," said Pillow.

"I am sure it will all be perfectly fine," Musette added. "Mrs. Supreme wouldn't let us travel on anything unsuitable."

As they sat in their basket, they could hear some people talking.

"Yes, all the papers are here," the driver said, and then came the rustle of papers.

"Just need to check their microchips," a woman said. "Then you can take them aboard. Would you pop them out of the car for me, luvie?"

The driver brought the basket out of the taxi and placed it on the tarmac. It was an extremely windy day and there was a chill in the air. Seagulls flew overhead, screeching for food.

Musette, looking around, feeling frightened at the vastness and strangeness of her surroundings.

The woman seemed to notice. "Now, now, little one, not to worry." She was a large lady with wispy blonde hair streaked with pink to frame her face. But she spoke kindly and gently lifted Musette into her arms. "I won't hurt you."

She took a scanner out of her pocket, held it over Musette's neck, and moved it round until she heard a *bleep*. On a display panel before her, a number popped up matching Musette's passport. The woman repeated the procedure with Pillow and Tibby. By the time all their passports had been checked and the cats cleared for boarding the ship, Sammy had appeared, ready to deliver the cats to the Captain.

""Hi there, you three," he said cheerfully, as the woman helped him place Pillow, Musette, and Tibby back into their basket. Once they were, Sammy said, "Let's get you settled, then," picked up the basket, nodded to the woman, and marched off down the metal gangway, embracing the basket with both arms to keep it steady.

As Sammy carried the cats onto the ship, they could hear the beats and hums of the large vessel, which sounded like a big cutlery drawer being opened and closed. And human voices echoed along the great passageways as if they were suspended in the air.

Finally, Sammy reached the Captain's cabin and knocked on the door four times.

"Come in!" shouted the Captain. But Sammy couldn't hear him. "Come in," shouted the captain again, but still Sammy didn't hear. The Captain radioed him.

"Oops," said Sammy as he put the cats down onto the floor. "I'm popular today." He took out his radio. "Yes, I'm outside your cabin, Captain," he said. "It's weird you're radioing me."

"No, Sammy," said the Captain, "there's nothing weird about it. Didn't you hear me calling out to you?"

"No, sir. I didn't hear anything," Sammy said, and scratched his head.

"That's because you're going deaf from wearing those stupid headphones and listening to such loud music! Would you just come in?" said the captain in an exasperated tone.

Sammy entered the Captain's cabin and once inside, placed the basket onto a tabletop.

When the basket was opened, Pillow, Musette, and Tibby looked up and got their first glimpse of the Captain. A tall, slim man with grey hair, he seemed very nice. "Hello, you furry things. Welcome aboard the *Golden Sun*. You're a lovely bunch, aren't you?" he said peering into the basket.

"Okay, Sammy, they need to go upstairs to the main deck. But I will also be taking care of them personally as I promised my friends. Pretend you didn't hear that," he said, and gave Sammy a wink.

10

CABIN CAPERS

Sammy left the Captain's cabin and headed for the main deck, which was two flights up. Some of the ship's cargo was kept there, as well as on the very bottom deck of the ship. Mrs. Supreme had insisted that the cats be kept outside since being cooped up inside, without fresh air, would make them unhappy. The Captain agreed and told the Supremes he would have one of the containers used for livestock adapted into a comfortable shipboard carrier for the cats.

As Sammy reached the door leading to the deck, the air became fresh and crisp. He stepped onto the deck, which held the cargo winches used to lift containers high into the air as they were taken on and off the ship.

"Lordy me," said Musette, peering through the basket. "Look at the height of those long things."

"Yes, they're like giant fishing rods," added Tibby.

"I hope they don't try and lift you off the ship with one of those, Tibby." Pillow laughed.

"Very funny," Tibby said with a shake of his head. "I do hope we will have some food soon. I am so hungry."

Suddenly Sammy came to a stop before a large, portable pen. "Here you are, then, mates, your new accommodations!"

The container was long and rectangular, made entirely from solid metal with high, solid, rigid walls. It was designed to be stacked like a giant Lego brick atop others, and a top could be added if needed. As the Captain had promised, the pen had been especially modified for the cats. Inside the pen, at the far end, was a large, wooden house with a cat flap, which would offer shelter from the harsh winds and rain that could quickly appear out at sea.

Sammy opened the container's large metal door and stepped inside. When he opened the basket, all three cats jumped straight out and looked around.

"This is most adequate," said Tibby.

"Yes, it's a huge space to run around in," Pillow added. "Look, there's a wooden house. Let's see what's inside. After you, Musette," he said like the perfect gentleman he was.

Musette skipped inside the little house first, followed by Pillow and Tibby. There was soft bedding and plenty of room in which to walk around. Three metal bowls filled with lightly poached salmon mixed with some little cat biscuits awaited them, along with a big bowl of milk.

All three headed straight to the dishes, sniffed the food, and agreed it smelled delicious. They gulped away, forgetting their surroundings and enjoying their lovely meal.

Once full of food, they lapped up the milk until the bowl was dry. Only then did they notice that Sammy was gone, for he'd headed back to work. So, they began to further investigate their new surroundings.

"Comfy bed," said Tibby, "and plenty of space, too, for all of us."

"Yes," Pillow agreed. "Let's see what's outside." He headed towards the door and pushed through to the other side. He found himself in the large enclosure, in the fresh air. Tibby poked his head through the large plastic flap next, followed by Musette.

Outside there wasn't much to see, just metal walls and a sky so cold and filled with clouds it was more white than blue.

But the ground under the cats' paws was softly padded and comfortable.

"Oh my," said Musette. "Smell that sea air. It's like the air from the gods."

"I think we are going to be fine here during our journey," said Pillow. "Delicious food, a wonderful bed, and good company." He looked at Musette with a glint in his eye.

"You've just described a cruise, Pillow," Tibby explained. "Humans do this for a holiday. They go on ships for weeks."

"A while ago you said it was no QE2, Tibby," Musette smirked. "I'm not the least bit surprised at your change of attitude now that you have stuffed your face!"

"I simply meant this ship doesn't resemble our dear Queen's vessel. But now I see it as a more of a Richard Branson ship, cool, trendy, and cat friendly."

Musette rolled her eyes, and then skipped back inside to get snug on the lovely bed that stretched across the floor. She was feeling a little tired from the long day. And since it was now going dark, she wanted to settle into her temporary home.

Pillow and Tibby, however, stayed outside, keen to explore further. But after sniffing around, from corner to corner, they soon decided to go inside as well.

"Ahh," said Tibby, stretching out like a long elastic band, "this is a lovely room."

"Sure is," said Pillow who was now curled up next to Musette. "Good night, old boy."

"Good night," Tibby said and yawned.

They woke early to the sound of the ocean. Waves gently caressed the ship as it sailed powerfully along. This movement was calming and agreed with all three cats. They woke, stretched, and ventured outside.

"I think we may just be seafaring cats," said Tibby.

Seagulls soared overhead, chattering almost in rhythm with the sound of the waves, as if talking to the sea itself. The sun was bright, warming the cats like a big, warm blanket.

"Ohhhh," Musette groaned with pleasure. "Do you think Hong Kong will be like this, warm and relaxing?"

"I do indeed," said Tibby. "I happen to know a lot about Hong Kong. I saw many things about it because Mrs. Maple and I used to watch an awful lot of television together. Only the interesting and informative channels, of course."

"Yes, I can tell," Musette said, looking at Tibby's large stomach.

A rather musical sounding bell rang.

"Ah, someone's getting married right now somewhere in the world," Pillow announced.

"You old romantic," said Musette, smiling.

"Isn't that why you married me, darling?" he asked.

Tibby cleared his throat, feeling a bit like a gooseberry. Then he gazed up at the large white gulls circling overhead. "I wouldn't want to take on one of those birds. Why, look at the size of them!"

"They are rather large." Pillow squinted as he stared into the sky.

"I wonder where we are now," said Musette with a swish of her tail.

CAPTAIN CATASTIC

Up on the bridge, the Captain was busy with his daily tasks. He had spent many years on ships, and he took great responsibility for every aspect of his vessel. He enjoyed standing watch at the helm, and was always alert, bright, and breezy. As he stood in front of all the ship's dials and gazed out to sea, he began to wonder how the Supremes' cats were doing. So, he asked his second officer to take over at the helm so he could pay the cats a visit. Then he would be able to call the Supremes and reassure them that their animals were doing fine.

When the Captain arrived at the big pen up on the main deck, he opened the door and found the three cats basking in the sun. "Hello, little fellas. How are you doing?" he asked.

At the sound of the Captain's voice, all three rushed to him. He knelt down so he could stroke each cat. Soon the sounds of contented purring were in tune with the rhythm of the ship.

"Well, it's good to see you all looking fine and content. I do hope you're more than happy with our chef's cooking. He has been told to prepare you fresh fish and chicken each day. That's much better than dry biscuits, eh, fellas?"

The cats were enjoying the company of a human, especially the Captain's kind hands and soft words. The only thing they missed right now was being able to take the kind of good, long stroll they used to take around their neighborhood in Beaconsfield.

"I must get back to work now, but I'll see you again soon."

With that, the Captain closed the cage and departed.

Back on the bridge, the Captain called Mr. Supreme. "Hello," he said, when Mr. Supreme answered the phone. "How are you and how was your flight? I guess you arrived safely?"

"Oh, it was all right. A bit of a drag, really, but we got through it," answered Mr. Supreme in his usually cheerful tone.

"What do you think of Hong Kong then?" asked the Captain.

"It's fine. I mean, it's really quite different, but we're getting adjusted and I am making money and that can't be a bad thing, can it?"

"Not at all," said the Captain and laughed. "Look, just thought I'd update you on the cats. They're doing fine, and they're all happy, content, and well fed," he said. Since he had taken a picture on his phone of the three of the cats lying in the sun looking very relaxed, he added, "I'll send you a photo of them."

"Please do," said Mr. Supreme. "That will keep the wife happy. She hasn't stopped talking about them since we got here!"

"Ahhh, bless her, she is a good woman," said the Captain.

"I can't thank you enough, Joe," said Mr. Supreme. "And we are looking forward to seeing you here in Hong Kong. It will be lovely to catch up."

"We've sailed out of Egypt and are heading toward Malaysia," the Captain informed. "It's been a very calm crossing and we are not expecting any bad weather, so expect to see us in two weeks. And I will give you another call in a few days."

"Fantastic," said Mr. Supreme. "Again, we can't thank you enough. Talk to you soon, then. Goodbye for now."

The Captain hung up and headed back to the bridge to resume his position. He decided he would stay at the helm for another four hours, after which he would bring the cats to his cabin for a while. He would appreciate the company; it would be good to have them around. Plus, the Captain never broke a promise.

After the Captain had left, the cats returned to the large enclosure to bask in the sun. But the excitement of their new surroundings was wearing a little thin and boredom was beginning to set in.

"Oh, how I long for a stroll around the garden, don't you, Pillow?" Tibby asked. "Imagine the lovely damp grass beneath our paws. I must admit, I am beginning to wish this voyage would fast forward us to Hong Kong."

"Me, too," said Musette. "I just want to sit on Mrs. Supreme's lap for a while. That's what I long for, nothing more than that."

Pillow was feeling fed up, too. He hadn't spent any time alone with Musette and was now getting a bit of cabin fever. They had been sailing for over a week and a half, so the novelty of good food and sea air was wearing thin.

"Come on, let's play a game," Tibby began. "Oh, wait. Here's the Captain again."

Indeed, the Captain had appeared and was now unlocking the door of the pen. He had the cats' basket with him, which surprised them.

"Do you think we're nearly there?" Musette looked excited.

"We can't be," replied Tibby, a bit puzzled. "We have at least another ten to fourteen days of sailing according to my calculations."

"Okay, little fellas, let's get you all in here," the Captain said, and then picked up and gently placed each cat into the basket.

Then he turned and, with basket firmly in hand, proceeded down a very long corridor. The cats could hear the clanging and banging of crewmembers busy with their work, mixed with the creaky, squeaky noises of the ship.

After what seemed like hours, the Captain stopped at his cabin door, which he slowly opened. Entering the room, he immediately set the basket down and opened it. The tops of the three cats' heads popped up, causing the Captain to chuckle.

"Come on, then, out you go. Nothing to be afraid of," he urged, and slowly the cats crawled out of the basket and looked around.

They found themselves in a spacious and comfortable-looking room, complete with a long, plush sofa attached to one wall. In front of the sofa sat a television set.

"Oh my! Just when you think things can't get any better, look where we are now!" Tibby exclaimed.

"Don't you mean 'worse'?" Musette asked, but Tibby was too busy exploring to respond.

All three of them crept about the room, looking behind the table and chairs. It all seemed very basic, yet spacious and comfortable. There was even a separate bathroom into which Pillow poked his head.

"That's where your litter tray's going to be," the Captain told them. "So, you'd best get used to going in there or you'll be out of here before you can say ship ahoy!"

"Everyone use it!" Tibby ordered. "Mrs. Supreme may have turned a blind eye, but the Captain certainly won't!"

"How dare you!" said Musette.

"I'm saying nothing," Tibby informed as Pillow looked quite embarrassed.

The Captain sat down on the sofa and switched on the television. He sighed and flicked away through the channels. He did this several times, which made Tibby feel quite dizzy. Finally, the Captain settled on a news channel.

"Ahh," Tibby said, pleased. "I do like to keep up with current affairs."

"Don't we know it," said Musette. "Personally, I miss Beaconsfield's news, or at least your interpretation of it."

"I was nothing less than a journalist, Musette. My reports weren't gossip, and without them, every day in Beaconsfield would have been quite dull."

"Well, I give you that," said Pillow, sniggering.

Relieved to be in the comfort of the Captain's lounge, the three cats got cozy. Thanks to the sounds of people coming from the television, they almost felt as if they were back home in Beaconsfield.

The Captain went over to his office desk and radioed Sammy. "Hello, young man. Can you go to the animal enclosure and bring me the cats' litter tray and their feeding bowls? I'm going to keep them here with me in my cabin for a bit. Can you do it now, Sammy? Who knows, they may need to spend a penny."

"Aye aye, Captain," Sammy said in his usual cheerful tone. "I'll get right to it!"

Aye aye, indeed, the Captain thought and chuckled. He did like Sammy an awful lot, especially his cheeky ways, which were so amusing.

Five minutes later, there was a knock at the door. In came Sammy, hands full, the cat tray in one hand, and a bag of cat litter under his arm. He placed them on the bathroom floor.

"I'll go now and get the bowls, sir," he told the Captain.

"Okay, Sammy. Pass by the kitchen on your way back. Have the chef put some food in a container. That will save you another trip."

"Cool," said Sammy, and off he went whistling a merry tune.

"Sunny days," said Musette. "It looks like we have been upgraded."

"We certainly have." Pillow looked very pleased.

The Captain sat back down again. "Come on, little fellas, sit here next to me." He patted the cushioned seat. Pillow and Musette sprang straight up onto the sofa, purring loudly, but Tibby remained on the floor.

The Captain picked Tibby up. "You're a heavy one, aren't you?" He plunked Tibby onto his lap.

Tibby looked at Musette. "Don't say a word, young lady."

"I wasn't going to," she said with a grin.

Pillow lay beside the Captain's thigh with Musette next to him. All four of them watched the news.

"It's a cruel world," said the Captain, with a shake of his head. "It's a cruel world, indeed."

As the news continued, the Captain, followed by the cats, started to nod off. Soon all four of them were fast asleep, breathing to the ship's motion. Then a knock at the door woke them.

"Captain, I'm back," Sammy called out.

"Ehhh, yes, Sammy, come in. I must have dozed off." The Captain slowly stood up, stretching, rubbing his neck, and yawning. When Sammy entered, his arms again full, the Captain directed him toward the small office tucked away at the side of the room. "You can put their bowls down there for now, Sammy. Oh, something looks nice," he said, peering into them.

"Yeah, it is," said Sammy. "Roast beef chopped up nicely. I also brought a carton of milk. I thought you could fill up their bowls when you need to."

"Good thinking, young man. I don't think they're going to be any trouble, do you, Sammy?"

"No, sir. Look at them, bless their little paws, what trouble could they possibly cause? Good night, Captain," Sammy said and left.

The Captain brushed himself down, checking his smart, crisp white shirt for any cat hairs. Then he peered in the mirror, checking his teeth. "You're a good-looking man," he said out loud, and then winked at himself.

"I'm going to leave the television on for you three," the Captain said, "but let's find something more suitable." He flicked through the channels, thinking, *I bet they don't want to keep watching the news. You can only take so much of that!* He stopped on the Disney Channel, and turned to Pillow, Musette, and Tibby. "I think you'll enjoy this, little fellas. I'll see you later. Don't go getting up to any mischief, and don't forget to use the cat tray." And with another wink, he turned and left the cabin.

"Oh, splish splash," said Musette with an indignant tone. "Why does he say that? It's so uncouth."

"I know why," said Tibby, looking right at Pillow.

The days passed pleasantly as the cats settled into their new cabin, enjoying the television, the sofa, and the Captain's visits. They were fed at the same time every day and the chef provided them delicious food. Sammy emptied their litter tray as often as he could, since that chore made the Captain rather queasy.

So, all was good.

LET'S GO OUT TO PLAY

I t was early in the morning and Sammy was back in the Captain's cabin again. "Good morning, folks, how're you doing today?" he asked in his usual cheerful manner.

All three cats were pleased to see Sammy, who always arrived with fresh food and a bounce in his step. "It's kippers this morning mixed with some rice," he announced. "Hope you like it ... well, that's silly to say. You seem to like everything, especially you, Tibby!" And with that, Sammy bent down to stroke Tibby's cuddly sides. "Good on you, mate, you fill your boots, ehh?"

"Fill your boots," Musette chuckled.

"And your hat and your coat, too!" Pillow laughed.

"Ha ha, very amusing," said Tibby. "You're quite the double act, aren't you two? I'll have you know I'm a fine fellow of a cat, hearty and well built. I can turn this into muscle overnight," he said patting his stomach.

"Really?" said Pillow. "The only thing you could turn overnight is this ship!"

Musette and Pillow laughed and laughed. "Stop!" cried Musette. "You're making my sides ache, Pillow!"

"And my head!" said Tibby, rolling his eyes.

Sammy's phone rang. "Hello? Yeah, I'm good, how are things with you? ... Hold on, I can't hear you over the TV. Wait a sec, I'm gonna have to go outside." And he went outside into the corridor to continue chatting, the cats watching him, since he hadn't closed the door.

After a few minutes, Sammy suddenly remembered he had to be at the bridge. "Gotta go, mate. Call me later!" And off Sammy went, running down the corridor, leaving the door to the Captain's cabin wide open.

Pillow moved over to the door, poked his head out, and looked down the long corridor. "Wow! Come and look at this, Tibby."

"Oh, fishcakes," Tibby said, but he moved to Pillow's side and peered out. "It's like a long pathway."

"Do you fancy a stroll?" Pillow asked.

"I don't know." Tibby felt a bit reluctant. "What if someone sees us? They could put us back in lower class, and I really like it here."

"Oh, don't be so dull, old boy. Musette, what do you think?" Pillow asked.

"I'm with Tibby on this one," she said, peering around the corner of the door now, too. "Uggg, it's not that interesting, it's just a long green corridor with lots of pipes and metal. No thank you. I'm staying put."

"Well, I'm not," said Pillow. "I want to go and look around. I think it will be fun," and he stepped outside. He ran down the corridor very fast and then he ran all the way back again.

"This is great" he shouted, "I haven't done this for weeks! It feels wonderful to be free! Come on, join me! Don't be boring!"

Tibby stepped outside. "Oh, to be young and foolish," he said, strolling down the long corridor, stopping to stretch and yawn every few steps. *But this does feel good,* he thought to himself.

"Don't overdo it now, Tibby," Pillow said with a smirk.

Suddenly, Musette rushed past Tibby, chasing after Pillow. When she caught up with him, she jumped on his back. Together they rolled around, pawing at each other playfully, as the floor beneath them hummed like a giant bumblebee from the power of the ship's engines.

Tibby shook his head at Pillow's and Musette's antics. But it did feel so good to be outside of the cabin, free, and with so much space.

Pillow felt quite brave now. "Let's see what's through here."

With Musette, and then Tibby following, Pillow led them to a flight of metal stairs. Through the large spaces between each step of the stairs, the floor below was visible.

"It looks scary," said Musette. "I don't think I can climb up them."

"Oh, yes you can. It'll be easy. Watch me." And Pillow started skipping up the stairs, one by one.

"Hold on, I'm coming, too!" Tibby said, leaving Musette behind.

"Fishcakes, so much for chivalry!" Musette complained, and she leapt onto the metal step, effortlessly following Tibby and Pillow, although she didn't look down once.

PICK A LETTER

At the top of the stairs they came to another corridor. This led them into a massive room with silver pipes twisting and turning like long frozen snakes that seemed to go on forever. There were huge funnels covered in foil with big metal boxes, which sounded like washing machines on a fast spin.

"I don't like it in here," said Musette. She could barely hear herself.

"LET'S GO, THEN!" shouted Pillow very loudly.

"This way! Let's follow the yellow lines on the floor. They must lead somewhere less noisy," Tibby suggested.

So, all three hurried along, following the yellow lines painted on the floor. They soon found themselves yet in another corridor, which was a lot quieter.

Pillow, still leading the way, reached another set of metal stairs. "Let's go up," he said.

"Hold on, let's read this sign," Tibby said. "G F E D C A. Do you want to pick a letter?"

"I don't know," replied Musette. "We don't know what they mean. And I just want to get back to the Captain's room. The noise is so tinny here, and I'm getting fed up with the jerks." Seeing the looks on Pillow's and Tibby's faces, Musette added, "I meant the jerks of the boat. Not you two!"

"Very funny, Musette. Okay, we can go back. Do you agree, Tibby?" Pillow asked.

"Yes, but I really would like to take a quick peek at the

galley first."

"Oh, full-fat milk, you would," muttered Musette.

"Look!" Tibby pointed to a white board. "The galley is just up one more flight of stairs. Come on, what do say, Pillow?"

"Okay, why not. I'm feeling a bit peckish myself." Pillow turned to look at Musette.

"Oh, whatever," she said with a sigh.

And the three cats climbed the stairs, leaping lightly from step to step until they had reached the next deck. As they approached the galley with Tibby leading the way, he stopped abruptly. "Hold on, there's someone in there." And since the galley door was ajar, Tibby peered into the room.

He saw the chef, clad all in white, standing at a long metal work surface, banging and clanging about with saucepans and muttering in French. Everything in the room was the same color, including the big cookers and hobs. And everything was terribly clean and shiny. Tibby felt he was looking into a room filled with mirrors.

He turned to Musette and Tibby, whispering, "We have to be very careful. We don't want to be seen. Look, there's a sign reading, 'Provisions.' That must be where they keep the food. Come on," he said excitedly.

Pillow and Musette crept behind him until they reached wooden shelves filled with tins, containers, and vegetables.

"Look over there," Tibby said. "Those must be the fridges. Doesn't look like we could ever open one, though."

"No, but don't be too disappointed, Tibby," Pillow said. "We're being fed and fed well. Let's get back to our cabin before the Captain returns or Sammy comes back to check on us."

"Agreed," said Tibby.

"This way then," Musette said and headed back toward the center of the kitchen.

The chef, who was still there, was now rubbing his head.

"He is very thin for a chef," Tibby muttered.

"Never trust a thin chef," whispered Pillow.

"I wouldn't, but he is an amazing cook," Musette said.

"Yes, he is, that's for sure. Great minds think alike," replied Tibby.

"What's that got to do with anything?" Pillow asked.

"Oh, never mind. It's only wasted," huffed Tibby.

"And what do you mean by that?" snapped Musette.

"Shhhh, someone will hear us. Come on, quickly, while he's not looking," Pillow hissed.

Tibby and Musette crept past the kitchen, heading back towards the stairs. Now they suddenly realized there were two sets, one leading left and the other right.

"I don't remember which one we came up." Tibby rubbed his head, trying to think.

"I do. It's the right one. See, there's the board we read with all the letters on it," said Pillow.

"It is indeed," said Tibby. "So onwards and downwards. Come on, Musette, do hurry as we really need to get back."

"I'm coming as fast as I can!"

They headed down to the deck below. Going down the metal stairs was scary because they could see right through the wide gaps between each step. When they reached the bottom, a long white corridor stretched out before them.

"I am sure our corridor was green, not white," said Tibby.

"No, it was green." Pillow sounded confident.

They continued down the long, narrow passage, which seemed to go on forever. And then they came to a door, but it wasn't open.

"We can't get through here," Tibby grumbled. "There's no way can we push that open. And it's probably locked anyway."

"We'll just have to head back and find another way, then." Pillow tried to sound sure, but he was feeling slightly concerned.

"Don't panic. It will all be fine," Tibby added brightly.

"Hold on a minute. We need to stop and think where we are first," said Pillow.

"Yes, you're right. We need to find a point we all recognize, so we can move on from there," Tibby stated.

"Let's go back up to the kitchen and then retrace our steps. Perhaps we should have taken the other stairway."

"Good idea, Pillow," said Musette, so off they went, running until they were again outside the galley.

It was even busier now for other workers had joined the chef. Some were chopping, some were stirring, and the chef was moving around like a clockwork mouse, shouting, "Not like zat! Like zis!" He grabbed the knife from one little man and began chopping furiously at parsley stalks, the sweat from his brow plopping onto the wooden chopping board.

"Yuk!" said Musette. "I'm glad we only get cooked food."

Then she, Pillow, and Tibby ran around to the other the side of the door.

"We need to go back down a deck, but this time let's take the stairs on the left side. That must be right," said Tibby.

"Left," said Pillow.

"Yes, I know!" Tibby shouted. "I meant left! Oh, never mind, just hurry up!"

They leapt down the steps, certain they would reach the room with all the funnels and long silver pipes. But at the bottom of the stairs, they only found closed doors and a long passageway. They decided to run as far down the passage as they could, hoping to find a way back to the Captain's cabin but they were only met by more stairways and more rooms filled with people working, chatting, and oblivious to the three of them.

Musette moaned.

"Look," said Pillow, "if we can't find our way back very soon, we will just have to return to the galley, walk in, make ourselves seen, and hope someone calls the Captain."

"And he'll send us straight back to lower class," Tibby grumbled.

"I don't care," said Musette. "At least we'll be safe and fed. Plus it can't be long now until we reach our new home."

"I agree with Musette." Pillow nodded. "Let's try one more flight of stairs, and if we can't find our cabin, we will surrender ourselves in the galley."

"Don't be so dramatic, Pillow," Tibby huffed. "We'll just stroll in and do our best to look cute and adorable."

Suddenly they heard whistling.

"Sammy!" Musette exclaimed. "That's Sammy!"

"Listen," Tibby added, "he's right through here…"

Indeed, Sammy was on his way to see the three of them for he was he was carrying a carton of milk. Up the stairs he came, headphones in place, listening to his favorite music and humming loudly as if he didn't have a care in the world. Then, since he had been inside all day, he decided to have a quick walk outside first for some fresh air, and maybe a walk along the main deck. This always helped him feel invigorated and inspired to write more in his journal.

And soon, without his even being aware of it, Pillow, Musette, and Tibby were right behind him.

HOLDING ON

Sammy opened the door to the main deck, and within seconds the three cats had squeezed through the small opening. But Sammy wasn't aware of this.

"Ohhh," he said, "it's going to be rough tonight. And too flipping cold for me." Shivering and clutching the carton of milk as if it were a hot water bottle, he stepped back inside and shut the big door, leaving the cats outside on the main deck where the wind was blowing fiercely.

"OH NO!" cried Musette, "now what are we going to do?!"

"Don't worry," said Pillow, "we will just go back inside."

The cold air seeped into their fur as if it had found somewhere to rest. The sea crashed against the ship, spraying water all over the main deck.

"We must stay close to the wall and stay together," Pillow said. "Musette, get between us so that Tibby and I can keep an eye on you. Nothing to panic about. It's just best we stick together, that's all."

"Good thinking," Pillow told Tibby.

"And we can make our way to the bridge. That's where the Captain always goes," said Tibby. "It's at the back end of the ship. I know this as I watched many a maritime program with my dear Mrs. Maple. This will allow the Captain to see us, or at least someone will. We can jump onto the ledge of the window since whoever's on the bridge looks through the window, and they'll spot us."

"Oh, I am so glad you had cable TV, Tibby," said Pillow. "It certainly had it uses.

The ship was now rocking from side to side, given the wind and the waves. Pillow, Tibby, and Musette struggled to stay upright, and they had trouble seeing. The harsh wind was sending so much water into the air it seemed to be raining. It was now dark as well, and it was hard to run since the deck was so slippery.

"This way!" said Tibby. "We want to head in the opposite direction of the containers." He pointed towards the tall mast with its flashing bright lights. "It will be just under there. Come on, it's not too far."

As they moved forward toward the bridge, the cats found every door they reached firmly closed.

"We have to keep going! We will never open any of them anyway," Tibby said. "Let's just keep going straight and we will reach it very soon."

There was no sign of anyone on the deck. The wind kept getting stronger, turning into a real gale, which made the sea dance even more dangerously, its waves growing higher by the second. The ship was riding the waves like a cowboy on a bucking horse, its nose above the waves one moment, and then plunging down into the foaming water the next.

"*OH MY!*" Musette cried. "I'm so wet! I don't like this. Pillow, I'm scared!"

"Don't be scared, Musette. Just keep as close to the wall as possible. It can't be long to go now," Pillow reassured her, but he knew they could easily be swept away in this storm.

"I don't think we should go any further," Tibby finally said. "It'll be safer to take shelter and sit it out until it's calm enough for us to get to the bridge."

Musette nodded and Pillow shouted, "Okay! There's a little, narrow spot up ahead that might give us some shelter. If we can get under one of those lifeboats, it will offer us some rest from the wind." Ahead, a small orange boat was hanging from a white hoist, which was used to ease the lifeboat overboard. The boat and winch were now swaying in the wind like an apple on a tree.

The cats continued straight ahead, but the wind was slowing them down and saltwater poured into their eyes, causing their vision to blur.

"HOLD ON, MUSETTE!" shouted Pillow. "We're nearly there!"

They reached the little lifeboat area Pillow had spotted. Under the boat hung a large, orange, plastic ring, which looked rather like a big cat toy. And next to it was a giant coil of rope they could latch onto with their claws. It looked like a big ball of string, but the rope was as thick as a big snake and very sturdy.

The cats tucked themselves in as tightly as possible behind the rope, close to the wall of the ship and out of the path of the harsh wind and water. Pillow and Tibby sandwiched Musette between them so firmly she could hardly see or breathe, but she was grateful to be safe.

"Are you okay, Tibby?" Pillow's voice was muffled.

"Yes, I'm fine." Tibby's fur was soaked through and he felt tired. "I say we stay here until the storm passes, even if we have to stay all night."

"All night?" groaned Musette.

She didn't know it, but Pillow and Tibby were struggling to keep hold of the rope since the wind was pushing at them with such force they could easily be blown away like kites. Pillow had hooked his left paw around the bend of the rope. His body ached because it was stretched like a bendy doll. Tibby had hooked his claws so far into the rope that as the wind pushed at him, he felt his claws might snap right off.

The rain continued to pour down, soaking into Pillow's and Tibby's fur. Although they didn't want Musette to know, they both regretted they had ever left the Captain's cabin.

When Tibby began to shiver, Pillow noticed. He was worried about Tibby, who was older and not as fit as Pillow. He knew he had to think of something. They could't stay here, for it was too dangerous and Tibby would soon run out of strength.

"Listen!" Pillow shouted. "We need to move! I am sure we can make it to the end of the deck, but we need to be fast."

"I don't know," Tibby said. "It's too risky. I can hold on. Please trust me on this, Pillow. I won't let Musette go, I promise with my whole heart. But if we try to move before the storm calms, we could get washed away."

Pillow could barely hear Tibby. Water was pounding down on them so hard, and the noise was so loud, it was as if Pillow and Tibby were a set of drums.

"What if we try and jump onto the lifeboat?" Pillow shouted back.

"No way! We would't make it, not in this, and they are far too high to reach!" Tibby yelled. "We just have to stop talking, conserve our strength, and hold on!"

So, they stayed there, hooked to the rope mostly by hope and prayer. They had been holding on for at least fifty minutes when the wind gradually started to ease off. The rain also began to fade as if it was being led away by the moon, which was now like a great torch glowing on the dark blue ocean below.

Pillow unhooked his paw, which felt stiff and painful. He arched his back to work out the kinks.

Tibby stretched out on his back as straight as he could to relax his muscles. He breathed deeply in and out, relieved to be out of danger.

Musette, who thought at one point she was going to suffocate, also breathed deeply. Thanks to Pillow and Tibby, she was dry, warm, and rested. "At last we can head to the bridge," she said. "They must be looking for us by now."

And, on the bridge, they were.

"I don't understand, Sammy," the Captain said sternly. "I left them in my cabin, but you're saying they're not there. How did they get out?"

Sammy spoke quietly, head down, for he couldn't look the Captain in the eye. "I left the door open by accident. I stepped into the corridor to take a phone call, and then I remembered I had to be with you, Captain. Knowing how you are with being punctual and all that, I was in such a rush to get back to you that I forgot to close the cabin door. I'm sorry, sir."

"Yes, you will be if you don't find them, young man. I promised my friends I would deliver those cats safely to their new home, and since we dock in three days, I suggest you stop talking and start looking!"

As Sammy turned and darted away, the Captain made an announcement over the speaker. "Will everyone please be on the lookout for three domestic cats roaming loose on the ship. If you see them, please approach with care. Do not scare them. Just secure them and contact me immediately. We are looking for them and they must be found."

Sammy headed for the Captain's cabin, upset and worried. *They must be around here somewhere* he thought. *The poor things will be hungry by now . . . Hungry! That's it! That's where they'll be. In the galley!*

And he turned around and headed for the kitchen.

THE STORM

"**Right,** are we ready then?" Pillow asked, feeling a bit better. He still ached but he knew it was important they get to the bridge.

"Yes, let's go," said Musette.

They unwound themselves from their hiding place and continued forward toward the bridge. The deck remained very wet and slippery, and it was difficult for them to balance. The ship was also still tilting and rocking, but not as harshly as before, so they were able to remain upright.

Pillow could see lights shining all around the front of the ship. He knew everything was going to be okay now since they would easily be seen. "You two stay here, and I'll jump onto the window ledge and get the Captain's attention," he told Musette and Tibby.

"That sounds like a good plan," said Tibby. He knew he would struggle to make a leap of that height. "I'll stay here with Musette. But do hurry, Pillow. It seems to be getting very blowy again."

Pillow leapt onto the ledge and peered through the bridge's big window. And there in front of him was the Captain. "It's the Captain! *I SEE HIM!*" Pillow shouted back to Tibby and Pillow.

At the same time, the Captain spotted Pillow and shouted, "Look! I've got one!" He radioed Sammy immediately. "I've got one, Sammy! I've got one! He's right in front of me, outside on the window ledge!" And the Captain watched as Pillow began to crawl along the window ledge, caressing its glass, and pushing himself against it as hard as he could.

"And where there's one, there will be two more!" Sammy cried out with relief. "I'm on my way back to the bridge, Captain!"

"Don't forget your life jacket, Sammy," the Captain ordered. "It's getting rough out there again, and no animal is worth dying for."

"Aye, aye, Captain!" And with that, Sammy grabbed a life jacket from a row above his head. The jackets were neatly hooked and lined up, and there was one for every member of crew on various levels of the ship. It was a yellow sleeveless jacket with a whistle attached. Sammy quickly put it on and raced toward the bridge.

Musette now shouted to Pillow, "Does the Captain see you?"

"Yes! He's peering at me through the window. He has't moved though . . ." Pillow yelled back.

"Don't worry. I bet someone's on their way up here now!" Tibby added.

"Of course, they are," said Pillow, and he hoped so, because things were changing again.

The wind had kicked up and the sea was becoming choppier. The ship rode the growing waves, bucking up and down again. Suddenly the cats heard a loud noise, which sounded like a herd of charging horses.

"What's that?" Musette cried out.

Pillow turned around, away from the window, but all he could see were white curls of frothy air, as if clouds had fallen from the sky and were aiming straight at him. Before he could do anything, a gush of cold water pounded him, pinning him to the window, flat as a pancake, and barely breathing from the force of it.

OVERBOARD

"**M**usette! Musette!" Tibby shouted. He couldn't see a thing. The air was now water, splattering and drenching him completely. "Musette! Musette! She's gone! She's gone!" Tibby screeched in Pillow's direction, retching up water.

Despite being splattered onto the window one moment, Pillow flew off the window ledge the next, his heart pounding and his stomach churning with dread. He rushed to the edge of the ship and leaned over. He spotted Musette in the sea, her paws frantically flapping at the waves.

Pillow looked around and spotted the orange plastic ring. "Tibby, help me with this!" he yelled, and then began pushing the ring up, trying to dislodge it from its holder. Tibby joined Pillow, and together they pushed and pushed at the ring, until it fell onto the deck.

"Push it to the edge with me!" Pillow yelled, and Tibby helped him. At the edge, Pillow turned to Tibby as he climbed onto the ring. Tibby's eyes went wide with understanding.

"Yes, push me off!" Pillow ordered. And so Tibby pushed the ring, which was much heavier now that Pillow was atop it. Tibby grunted, and shoved with all his might, and the ring, and Pillow, holding on as best he could, flew over the side of the ship.

When the ring hit the water, within range of Musette, Pillow screamed, "I'm coming, Musette!" Terrified she would go under, he held onto the ring and started kicking his way toward her.

Tibby, shaking all over, watched in terror. *They'll never make it back up here*. His heart was breaking. He couldn't stay on deck, not without them. So he counted, "One, two, three," and then jumped, screaming *"AHHHHHH!"* as he flew through the air.

He hit the water, which was so cold it knocked the breath right out of him. Luckily, he landed close to Pillow, and he kicked and pawed his way up to the surface, sputtering.

"Tibby! Don't make any *more* waves!" shouted Pillow. "Grab onto the ring. We need to get it over to Musette!"

Tibby paddled closer and grabbed the ring. Since it was made of fiberglass, his claws could latch onto the tiny scratches already on its surface thanks to the wear and tear of the ocean.

"Hold on, Musette! We're coming!" Pillow yelled over the roar of the waves and wind.

"Please, hurry," she said weakly, spitting out more water. She was so cold she thought she might pass out. Her teeth were chattering like castanets.

Tibby and Pillow were kicking their back paws as fast as they could while Pillow tried to steer the ring toward Musette with his front paws. "Nearly there!" he screamed, although his throat was tight and he felt numb not only from the cold, but from shock as well.

They finally reached Musette, and Pillow swam to her and lifted her up onto the ring. She sprawled out completely flat, all four of her paws dangling into the water, breathing heavily.

"WE NEED TO BALANCE THE RING, TIBBY, SO IT DOESN'T FLIP OVER!" Pillow yelled.

So Tibby dragged himself bit by bit around the ring, until he reached a spot directly opposite Pillow. When he latched onto it, Tibby felt the ring steady itself. But in his heart, he knew it was unlikely they would be rescued. The odds were against them. However, Tibby also knew the importance of staying mentally focused, since the will to live might be the only thing that could save them.

"Try and get onto the ring," Musette begged. "Please, Pillow, please, Tibby! You can't stay in the water, it's too cold!"

Pillow pulled himself up first, trying not to throw the ring off balance and send himself and Musette back into the sea. When he found the right spot, he positioned himself like Musette, lying flat atop the ring.

"Now you, Tibby. Come on, you must get up here!" Musette called out.

Tibby tried pulling himself up, but he couldn't lift his leg out of the water. "I can't," he said, "I just don't think I can do it." He again tried to throw his leg over the ring. This time he did it, but he couldn't bring the rest of his body along with. Cold and tired, he didn't have the strength. "I'll just stay here," he said weakly. "As long as you two are okay, that's what matters."

"You will NOT stay there!" Pillow yelled. "You're getting on this ring if I have to drag you onto it!" Pillow started to crawl backwards to where Tibby was hanging on. "Don't move, Musette. Just hang on. You may go under the water for a second or two, but hold on and don't let go!" Pillow ordered.

"Yes, yes, but just get Tibby," she said.

"Now listen, Tibby, I'm going to jump off the ring now," Pillow explained. "But don't you let go of it, either."

"I won't," Tibby said with determination.

Pillow jumped into the sea and swam under Tibby. He then pushed Tibby's legs upward until Tibby was on the ring. The ring became unsteady, and Musette's side of it rose out of the water, but Pillow quickly hauled himself back onto the ring. Given his added weight, the ring again became balanced and steady.

"Well, I'm no Captain Hook but I think we are heading into the Pacific Ocean," Tibby stated.

"I'm so thirsty," Musette said.

"It's the saltwater you swallowed," Tibby informed. "You must resist the temptation to drink anymore."

"I couldn't drink that, and what I did swallow, I certainly didn't mean to," Musette replied.

"We know, Musette," Pillow told her.

"Do you think we are going to die?" she asked.

"No darling, of course not," Pillow said. But secretly he was worried. He couldn't see a way out of this. All he could see at this moment was the ship, which was moving away from them and would soon disappear completely.

"Try not to worry, Musette," said Tibby. "It will be okay once the sun rises. I promise you, we will feel warm and dry. What's important now is that we stay on this ring. That's all we need to think about for now," he said, trying to sound reassuring.

On the ship, Sammy's face was as white as the caps of the wave as he stood before the Captain. "They're not anywhere, Captain. They're gone."

"I know, son," the Captain said gently. "Why don't you get some sleep now. Tomorrow will be a new day, and you'll have plenty of work to do."

"Do you think I should go outside and look for them?" Sammy asked.

"My dear, boy, there's not a person on this ship whose life is worth risking for a cat, not on my watch. Their time had come, and may God bless them. Now be off with you."

But after Sammy departed, the Captain stared out the bridge window for a long time, silent and lost in thought.

SUPREME SADNESS

The phone rang and Mr. Supreme answered it. After a moment, he called out to Mrs. Supreme, who was in the other room, "It's the Captain."

"Tell him hello for me," called back Mrs. Supreme.

"All right." Mr. Supreme turned his attention back to the phone call. "Oh … Oh, I see," he said. "No, no, please don't worry, Joe, it was an accident. We will see you when you get here. We can talk about it then," he said, very composed and matter of fact.

Mrs. Supreme appeared at the door of the room, and Mr. Supreme turned his back on her to finish the call.

"What happened, happened. And knowing those three, they probably jumped ship. Must have been the food! Seriously, you're too kind and too soft, Joe. Yes. We will see you soon. And truly, it doesn't matter. They're just cats."

Mr. Supreme put down the phone. He covered his face with his hands as his shoulders shook.

Mrs. Supreme moved to her husband and stroked his back. "What's the matter, darling? What is it? Tell me, please," she urged.

When Mr. Supreme looked at his wife, she saw tears streaming down his face. "It's the cats, love. They went missing from the ship during a storm. The Captain's not sure how. But they're not coming home."

Mrs. Supreme began to cry, too. She wept until she was so exhausted from crying that she eventually fell asleep. And she dreamt of her beautiful companions, happy, safe, and content.

When she woke in the morning, Mrs. Supreme knew in her heart that the cats would somehow be fine. She said her prayers, got dressed, and started to prepare breakfast.

The sun was rising, easing its way up above the horizon, as Sammy walked the top deck of the cargo ship, praying for a miracle. Heading for the bridge, he noticed one of the life rings was missing. *How did it get down from its holder? Where has it gone?* he wondered, but then he had an idea. And he ran to find the Captain.

After Sammy told the Captain his idea, the Captain thought for a moment, stroking his chin. "Well," he then said, "you never know, Sammy, you never know. Have you ever heard the expression 'three men and a boat'?"

"No." Sammy looked puzzled.

"Well, from now on it's 'three cats and a ring,'" the Captain said, thinking, *If this crazy idea gives Sammy some comfort, what harm can it do?*

Sammy left the bridge and walked back down the deck, his mind going ten to a dozen. *No, surely not*, he thought, *they couldn't have . . . could they?*

The Captain, who was a curious sort and liked to know everything, knew no one had been on deck during the storm to throw the ring overboard. He also knew that the ship's extra life rings were attached too firmly to their hangers to be blown off them even in the worst of weather. But the Captain did wonder where that ring had gone. So he made another announcement.

"Hi di hi, campers," he said. "We have a mystery on board our dear ship. The life ring from the top deck has gone missing. Any explanation, good or bad, as to its whereabouts will be accepted without question. Over and out."

Down in the galley, after the announcement was heard, the chef looked at his assistant and shook his head. "Ze cats are missing, now a life ring? I think ze Captain has been at ze gin again."

As Pillow, Musette, and Tibby lost sight of the ship, they realized they were alone at sea. At least it was light now, and they could see all around them. The air felt a little warmer and the chill had finally left their bodies. But they could only lie still. Any sudden movement might cause the ring to flip over, and water was not something they enjoyed. It felt unnatural, almost cruel to be this close to water. No cat ever went near water; it was simply not done. This was a situation all cats dreaded.

Tibby noticed that Musette was nodding off. "Stay awake, you can't sleep," he said.

"Oh, let her sleep," Pillow added feebly. "She could sleep on the edge of a dining room chair for hours. She won't fall off. Musette was born with more balance than a pair of scales."

"Fair enough," Tibby said and yawned.

"But don't you nod off. I don't fancy dragging you out of the sea again. I don't have the energy, so just stay put. And why did you jump, Tibby? You could have stayed on the ship. You would have been fine."

Tibby shrugged, not wanting to reveal his true feelings. "I just always fancied a cruise on one of those big cruise ships, so this was my opportunity."

Pillow grinned. "Oh, Tibby, you're so witty."

"One for all and all for one," Tibby said. "And now look at us, sailing the Pacific Ocean on a fancy raft. Who wouldn't want to do this?"

Pillow suddenly looked serious. "What are our chances? What chance do we have of surviving, Tibby? You can be honest with me. I want to make it as easy for Musette as I can, if you know what I mean . . . "

"Now just you listen to me, young man." Tibby lifted his head up. "We have every chance in the world. We just need to rest now and conserve our strength. Then we will think of a way to gather food. Do you know what's right beneath us?"

"Hmm. Let me think," said Pillow. "A big puddle?"

"Not funny," Tibby replied. "Fish. More fish than you ever dreamt of, so once we figure out how to balance this raft, I will catch us a beauty and we will feast on fresh fish, which will also prove us enough liquid to sustain us until we reach land, do you hear me?"

Pillow nodded, and they continued bobbing along on their bright orange raft as the sun beat down on them. Musette remained fast asleep, which was a blessing since her throat was as dry as sand and her beautiful, sleek fur was becoming as coarse as hay.

BREEZE

"**M**y throat's as dry as the Sahara," moaned Tibby. "I hope it rains, for I'd rather be wet than dried out like a desert."

Pillow felt the same way. "How long can we last without fresh water, Tibby?"

"Not long. Around three days tops. Maybe a few more."

Tibby and Pillow looked up to see seagulls circling above them. They were actually glad of the company. They watched as one bird, that was white as snow and twice Pillow's size, flew down and settled herself on top of the water to float there gently.

"We saw you on the ship when you were outside on the deck. However did you end up out here?" the gull asked.

"Oh, we fancied doing a bit of water sports," Tibby joked as Pillow rolled his eyes.

"I'm Breeze," said the seagull, "and this is my flock."

At this all the gulls circling overhead began to screak and call. The noise was loud but quite welcoming in the vast, lonely ocean.

"Musette, my Cattona, got swept off of the ship, and, well, here we all are. I'm Pillow and this is Tibby."

"Pleased to meet you," said Tibby.

"You're in the Pacific Ocean," Breeze informed.

"*HA!* I knew it!" Tibby was quite proud of himself.

"The wind is taking you towards the island, and by our navigation, you should be on shore by tonight," Breeze said.

"Shore?" piped up Musette, suddenly awake. "Did I hear you say 'shore'?"

"Yes," Breeze said. "Don't worry. You will be there soon."

"Oh, good. I'm so very thirsty." Musette sleepily rubbed her eyes.

"Do you know of the name of the island?" asked Tibby.

"Yes," said Breeze, "it is called Cataqueria Island."

"I haven't heard of that one before," Tibby said. "Mind you, there are so many of them I guess I couldn't possibly know them all."

"Oh, you will get to know this one," Breeze said with a smile. Just as Tibby was about to ask *Why*? Breeze called out to her flock. Suddenly they all came flying down like kites on a downspin, diving and disappearing right into the ocean. After a few seconds, fish began flying out of the sea, right toward Tibby, Pillow, and Musette.

"Grab some," shouted Breeze as her flock continued to fling the small, silver fish, which were wriggling like little mice, out of the water.

Musette quickly caught two fish, which she held in her mouth. Pillow almost laughed, but he turned to Tibby. "I'll catch, too, Tibby, while you watch the raft!" And Pillow began catching fish with both paws, crunching into their backs to stop them from wriggling, and collecting them between his legs. The raft jolted from side to side and splashed the cats with water thanks to this activity, but that didn't matter. At least they now had food.

Breeze's flock emerged from the water and flew back into the sky, squawking with delight at their fine catch.

"Enjoy! There's plenty to go around," Breeze told Pillow, Musette, and Tibby. "Maybe we'll catch up with you later." And with that, off she flew, disappearing with her flock.

"Thank you!" shouted Pillow, "Thank you!" He waved one paw while pushing a few fish toward Tibby. "Here you go. Dig in."

Well, I never," Tibby said, tucking into his fish. "You couldn't 'make it up, could you? What a sight!"

"I had never met a seagull before, not in person. I'd heard about them from cats that spent time on the coastline. And I feel so ashamed," Pillow admitted. "I always thought they were greedy and unkind."

"Well, you thought that about me!" Tibby commented.

"You know you shouldn't believe everything you hear or are told, Tibby. You must form your own opinions in life, and base them on the truth," Musette said. Then she added, with a sly grin, "Like in your Beaconsfield Journal. Remember? 'Coburn meets with the Vicar's cat for afternoon prayers.' That really was a classic! He was just looking for the church rat that, according to you, was a ghost from the past!"

"Well, no one ever caught it," Tibby said, defending himself, and missing the look shared between Musette and Pillow.

"That's because it lived in a cage and belonged to the Vicar. Honestly, Tibby, I wish I had an imagination like yours," Musette said, smiling.

"I did enjoy writing that," Tibby said with pride.

"Well, Coburn didn't," added Musette, "especially since Sassy thought he had gone to discuss their wedding!"

"Typical Sassy, wanting to get married in the church," laughed Pillow.

"I did wonder why Coburn hadn't been seen for weeks," said Tibby. "And I shouldn't have bothered with the missing bulleting."

"Don't even go there," said Musette. "That was another story!" She and Pillow knew that most of Beaconsfield's cats

73

read Tibby's journal because it contained so much gossip and silliness.

They continued to drift along in the water. Despite no longer feeling hungry, they still felt thirsty.

"I hope Breeze is right about us reaching an island soon, because I do wish I had some fresh water," said Musette.

"I'm sure Breeze is right," Pillow stated with confidence. "She knows this ocean like we know our old neighborhood."

"This ocean is full of islands. I know that," Tibby added. "I've seen programs about the Pacific."

"You certainly did watch a lot of television with Mrs. Maple, didn't you?"

"I did indeed, Pillow, and it was most informative and extremely useful."

I hope some more of that information will be useful to us, Pillow thought.

Time passed and it felt as if it was getting hotter, perhaps because there was no shade to be found out at sea. Normally the cats loved the heat, but the problem was that they couldn't move around at all, so the sun beat down on them mercilessly.

Their raft did feel solid beneath them as it bobbed along, sometimes twirling in gentle circles like the car dodgems at a fairground. It would always right itself and continue bobbing along in the same direction thanks to the soft waves that seemed to gently guide it.

All three cats were lying still, not even talking. Pillow turned his head to check on Musette and found her lying flat and limp as a glove puppet. "Musette?" he said, but she didn't respond. "Musette, wake up," Pillow repeated, beginning to worry.

"I'm so tired," she groaned.

Tibby, who was lying with his eyes closed, popped one open at the concern in Pillow's voice. When Tibby looked at Musette, he felt worried for she didn't look well. But he said, not wanting to alarm Pillow, "She is just weary, Pillow. It's best that she sleeps. It won't do her any harm. She's had food, and the liquid in those little fish will keep all of us fine for a while yet."

"Do you think so?" Pillow asked while keeping his eye on Musette.

"Yes," said Tibby. He closed his eyes again, hoping Pillow wouldn't see the worry in them. "Remember, Pillow, we're all in shock. Yes, we've had food and we're warm and dry, but we had an exceptional experience. Now we have to stay calm and trust that Mother Nature will bring us safely to shore."

But Pillow didn't respond.

Tibby opened one eye and saw that Pillow was now sitting straight up. Balanced on the ring, he was still and staring into the distance.

"Pillow, are you, all right?" Tibby asked, opening his other eye, but staying in place, since he didn't want to rock their little boat. "Pillow?" he repeated. "Pillow? What is wrong?"

19

CATAQUERIA ISLAND

"**L**and! I can see land! Land!" Pillow exclaimed. "Look! Musette, look!"

But Musette only mumbled, and her lack of response told Tibby she was, indeed, very poorly. He turned to Pillow, "I think we should get this raft ashore as soon as possible."

Pillow nodded, and then he and Tibby rolled onto their stomachs, and positioned themselves so that their front legs were hanging over the side of the raft.

"On the count of three," Pillow told Tibby. "One, two, three!"

They plunged their paws into the water and began paddling as hard and fast as they could. The raft began to pick up speed.

"It may get more difficult as we get closer to shore," Tibby told Pillow. "And we don't want to be going against the tide, for we could be swept back out to sea."

"Okay," Pillow said, adding, "Did you learn that by watching television?"

"Why, I believe I did."

"I'm glad you did, Tibby, I'm glad you did," Pillow said.

And they paddled with their paws until their bones ached, but their spirits were as high as the sun.

"Keep going!" said Tibby.

"I will!" replied Pillow.

But after a few more seconds, Tibby, who was breathing hard, asked, "Can we have a rest now?"

"You just said keep going!" Pillow had stopped paddling, too.

"I know I did," said Tibby, catching his breath. "But I'm not as young and fit as I used to be. We will pick up speed again shortly. And as soon as we see the water getting lighter, that means it's getting shallower. And that means we're not far from the shore.

As they continued to paddle, both felt excited because they could see the island more clearly. They spotted tall palm trees and lush green plants reaching into the sky.

"I can't see any buildings," Pillow said.

"The island may not be inhabited by humans. I can't see any sign of life, not a harbor, not a boat, not anything. But it doesn't matter. We'll be able to have a stretch and a stroll, find fresh water, and later have a good sleep in that beautiful, warm sand."

"It looks like paradise from here," said Pillow.

"I'm sure it is," Tibby added.

Glancing at Musette, they both secretly hoped their wishes for the island would prove true, for, still asleep, she was looking more lifeless by the second.

"All right, Tibby, let's do this. One more big effort and we will be walking on soft sand."

"Okay," Tibby replied, taking a big breath. "I'm ready!"

Paws went back into the water, and with heads down and backs up, Tibby and Pillow stroked as hard as they could. But as they got nearer to the shore, they realized they were going back out into the ocean.

"We're in the undertow! It's no good!" Tibby cried. "We're going to have to swim to shore! Wake up Musette! Pillow, she'll have to swim as well because we're not strong enough to paddle against and beat the backwash tide!"

"Just leave her, Tibby! I will push us to shore." And before Tibby could say anything, Pillow jumped off the ring and into the sea. "Ahhh, it's warm! Come on in, Tibby, it feels lovely!"

"Really?" Tibby wondered if Pillow had sunstroke.

"Tibby, jump in. It won't take long for us to push the raft to shore!"

"All right, I trust you!" Tibby shouted and leapt into the sparkling blue water. He could see straight through it to the sandy bottom, which was covered with bright, glistening shells. "This does feel good!" he exclaimed. "It's cool, not cold, and very refreshing!"

"Who says cats don't like water?" Pillow laughed.

"I don't know if I'd go that far," Tibby spluttered, spitting out some water as he spoke.

"Let's push!"

"Okay!" Tibby said, for he was longing for a stroll on the beach.

They got behind the ring, placed their front paws on it, and started kicking furiously with their back legs, using every last bit of their strength and willpower.

Finally, they reached the shore, exhausted yet exhilarated to be on dry land.

"Wake up, Musette!" Pillow said excitedly. "Look, we made it, we're safe, and we're out of the ocean, my angel!"

Musette stirred and groaned. Although her throat was dry, her limbs ached, and she felt weak, she managed to stand up. She looked around, not quite sure where they were, for she could see sand and trees but nothing else.

"Stay here, Musette. Tibby and I will go find something to drink," Pillow said.

"That's what you need, Musette, and you'll feel as right as rain," Tibby told her.

Musette nodded and soon found herself alone. She could hear the waves embracing the sand, leaving frothy white edges. The water close to shore was the palest blue she had ever seen, paler even that Sassy's eyes. Musette stared back out to sea where the water was so much darker. The clouds on the horizon looked like marshmallow mountains, soft and inviting.

A tall palm tree stood near shore, leaning out toward the sea as if it wanted to jump in for a swim. With its dark green leaves, it reminded her of a giant Christmas decoration. She put her paw into the sand. The color of vanilla custard, it felt almost like sugar, and Musette enjoyed its soft feel.

She saw that the sky was a very different blue from England's. More vibrant and sparkling, it made everything appear beautiful, clear, and crisp.

The sun warmed her back, and she sighed. *Ahhhhh, this feels so good I could just stay here forever.* She closed her eyes, enjoying the feel of the warm sand, the peaceful sound of the waves breaking gently on the beach, and the cool breeze that brushed over her little face.

Is this what heaven is like? Musette wondered. *Are we in heaven?*

VINNIE

Vinnie grabbed the little mouse in one clean swoop. "Ah, breakfast," he said, grinning like a Cheshire cat, not that he bore any resemblance to one.

Vinnie was jet black, his coat shiny as a penny, his eyes as green as blades of fresh grass. His body was long, hard, lean, and solid. He had twenty-seven toes. No other cat on the island had or had ever seen this many perfectly manicured toes. Vinnie was very proud of his long, sharp, pointed claws. They were as long as silver needles, and Loops, his Cattona, would file them to a point for him. As part of his manicure, she would then rub coconut oil into his paws, being careful not to touch his hard, rough paw pads. She would finish by rubbing flint over his claws until they glistened like spears of ice.

Vinnie sat comfortably, crunching away, and gulping down his catch. "Ummm, very good, very good, indeed," he said in a voice that was deep, slow, and twisted.

Suddenly he held his strong, noble head high, and sniffed the warm air. "Hmmm," he said. He was quite sure an unfamiliar scent was circling about, a scent his nostrils were not accustomed to. He stretched his neck even higher above his bony shoulder blades, which poked out and looked a bit like the wings of a vulture.

Getting up, he began to follow the scent, weaving gracefully through tall reeds of yellow grass, continuing toward the beach, where the scent became stronger and stronger.

Vinnie moved precisely, quietly, and slowly. He stopped,

paused for a few seconds, and then stopped abruptly. All that moved now was his long tail. It moved side to side, like a deadly cobra. He peered through the long grass, and caught sight of Pillow, who was up a tree, trying to pull a coconut from a large cluster.

"Well, well, well," Vinnie hissed, as his back arched and his claws sprung out of his paw pads with a dangerous sounding *twhick*. "What's this? A strange Catton on my island?" Vinnie chuckled. "Look at the state of him. Ha! I would be shocked if he could open one of those puppies." Opening coconuts was easy for Vinnie, thanks to his metal-like claws.

He was just about to make his presence known when he spotted Tibby, dragging behind him a big coral reef fish.

"Well done! I am very impressed," Pillow shouted when he spotted Tibby.

Anyone can catch those, Vinnie thought. *But I am surprised that old, fat cat managed to do so.* Vinnie's snickering ended abruptly when he saw something else.

Musette came running out from behind one of the big sand dunes. She was feeling so much better after drinking the freshwater Pillow had found in a small spring near the shore. In fact, she felt so good that she had been making beds with feathers she found by the edge of the tropical forest. She looked vibrant, alive, and excited as she praised Tibby for their wonderful breakfast.

"My, my, my," Vinnie whispered to himself, "and what do we have here?"

TAKEN HOSTAGE

Vinnie watched Musette and schemed. "I may need a little back-up here, just to be on the safe side, not that I couldn't handle things myself. After all, that fat tabby is just a lump, although he may be as heavy as he looks. And as for monkey boy up the coconut tree, I could take him out easily. But the girl … ah, the girl …" Vinnie took a long, deep breath. "She's surely going to admire me."

Vinnie was very conceited, and to be fair he had every reason to be. He was a very powerful Catton. All the older girl kittens on the island seemed smitten with him, especially the Kit and Mixes, the young female cats who were looking for a Catton of their own. And Vinnie, after all, was mean, lean, strong, and tall. Plus, nobody dared mess with him because of his knife-like claws.

After watching Musette a bit longer, Vinnie backed away slowly, keeping low to the ground so as not to be seen. As soon as it was safe to do so, he sprang up and ran back to tell the others, excited about this chance to prove his power and position to all the members of the colony.

Vinnie also loved a drama. He spent most of his days stirring up trouble amongst the other Cattons whilst strutting about in front of the Kit and Mixes, teasing them with his smug face and his glistening grass-green eyes.

Back at the colony, which was about half a mile inland from the shore, Vinnie immediately called a meeting. The other cats gathered around, some fat, some thin, some ugly, others bony, battered or scarred, but they all did what Vinnie wanted. They knew he was dangerous, fearless, and could easily strike out at them.

Danny was Vinnie's right-hand cat, and, like Vinnie, he was hard, fearless, and no one dared question him. Danny was white, orange, and grey, with a long, pointed face, and dirty green eyes the color of a wet toad.

"What's happening?" Danny asked Vinnie.

"We have visitors. Three of them, two males and one female, and a pretty one at that," Vinnie grinned. "They're down by the beach making a nice little home for themselves. I want you and a few of the boys to go down there with me, round them up, and bring them back here, alive. And then take the girl straight to my Loops. She can take care of her for me," and he grinned in his sneaky way.

Danny laughed. "Vinnie, you're the head catton, you really are. But won't Loops—"

Vinnie cut Danny off with a wave of his paw.

Loops was Vinnie's Cattona. She was a tiny, very pretty black and white tabby with eyes as pale blue as the sea. She had been Vinnie's Cattona for two years. She loved him deeply and understood that a Catton of his position had privileges. She had turned a blind eye to Vinnie's Kit and Mixes, always hoping that the next one Vinny paid attention to would be the last. Loops quietly longed for him to stop chatting with the unattached females and just pay attention her and only her. Vinnie, however, loved flirting and loved the adoration from the young females, although Loops did give the best manicures on the island. Danny often told Vinnie, "I know you love Loops," but Vinnie would shriek, *"LOVE? WHAT IS LOVE, YOU JABBERING FOOL?"* So Loops never said a word to Vinnie, for she knew her place, and knew that a whiny

Cattona would end up a very lonely Cattona.

Now, given Vinnie's order, Danny shrugged. "I'll get on it."

The other male cats in the colony sat around, waiting to see what was going on. Only a few of them were mean and nasty enough to be chosen to fulfill Vinnie's orders. Most of the cats went about their days taking care of their families and avoiding Vinnie, who was too dangerous to challenge. Some had thought about it and had even held secret meetings to discuss the possibility of bringing Vinnie down a notch. But they all reached the same conclusion again and again. They couldn't stand up to Vinnie for if anything happened to them, there'd be no one to take care of their families.

Danny pointed his thick, hardened paws at three cats: Mickey, Vernon, and Spit, who were sitting together, chewing their tobacco leaves. "All right, boys," Danny said, "let's go and get some action!"

Mickey was a tall, thin cat with black and white stripes across his long, scraggly body. His face was shaped like a narrow rectangle and covered in scars. Wiry whiskers stuck out in every direction from his pink nose. Mickey liked Danny because he had a big family, and Mickey especially liked Danny's sister Suzy Wong, who he intended to cross paws with. So he was happy he got on well with Danny, and they both enjoyed their wicked banter. As bad as they were, family came first for Danny and Mickey.

Danny also had a sister named Suzy Wing, who looked very much like Suzy Wong but was very different in personality. Suzy Wing was married to Vernon, who was as dull as his wife. While Suzy Wong was always smiling and skipping around, Suzy Wing mostly frowned and dragged her feet for she was slow to react to anything that moved, other than someone's mouth. She did love to have a chat and share gossip.

Vernon and Spit were brothers. They were both as orange as ginger-nut biscuits with different golden shades woven through their fur, making them appear like mottled cake mix. Everyone called them the "ginger nuts," hard on the outside and soft in the middle. They spent most of their time working security, pacing the grounds day and night, and checking that all the other Cattons were doing their work. Vernon and Spit ran a tight ship, but they were fair and decent with the other Cataquerians. As long as everyone obeyed, Vernon and Spit would harm no one.

Tibby was feeling quite proud of himself. He had caught a fish, and had even managed to leap on a bird, which provided more feathers for warmth and comfort, as well as what would be a fine lunch that day. Despite having eaten only tinned food for so long, Tibby always thought fresh food was so much healthier. He had watched many documentaries and health programs with Mrs. Maple. He considered himself something of an expert on nutrition, as well as other medical matters.

He was also creating a calendar on a long tall palm tree. He had worked out that today was Sunday, and so made one mark on the tree. Then he added six more marks and crossed out the first one (Sunday) so he could keep track of the days. He had already decided to write his autobiography when he was rescued from this island, which, since he was an optimist, he felt would be soon.

Tibby gazed out to sea, deep in thought. *I'm like Robinson Crusoe, who will be saved by a passing ship, and I'll go down in history as a cat of all lands, a Bear Grylls of the cat world, a captain of all cats.*

As Tibby imagined his name in books, something leapt on him and dragged him down into the sand.

"Ahhhhh! Get off me, you clumsy oaf! I'm getting sand all over me!" Tibby complained, thinking Pillow was being quite silly.

But when Tibby was roughly turned over onto his back, he found himself staring up at Danny. He leapt onto Tibby's big stomach, and spread his paws evenly over Tibby, like a tent.

"Ugh! I'm a c-c-cat! L-l-look, I'm a c-c-cat!" Tibby was so terrified that he stuttered. "I know I am a bit on the large side, but I'm a cat," he added feebly.

"Yeah," Danny hissed, "and we don't like strangers just strolling into our territory. You've got some explaining to do."

"Danny, you stay here with fat boy," Vinnie ordered. "Mickey, Vernon, and Spit, come with me. We'll get the others."

"What others?" Tibby asked, trying to save his friends. "I am here all alone."

"Ahh, how touching," Danny sneered. "Now *SHUT UP*."

Vinnie and the three other Cattons crept towards the beach. They could see two cats curled up fast asleep, snuggled together in a soft golden sand dune. With a wave of his paw, Vinnie ordered the others to follow him as he silently advanced on the two sleepers.

"How sweet," said Spit, now standing over Pillow and Musette. With a smile that showed his broken yellow teeth, Spit stuck out his long, bent paw and pushed it into Pillow's head.

Pillow flicked the paw away. "Not now, darling, I'm dead beat."

Vernon laughed. "Not now, darling, I'm dead beat," he said

in a mocking tone. Mickey and Spit sniggered while moving their tails aggressively.

Pillow suddenly jumped up, claws spread wide open, his soft back arched like a matador about to be charged by a bull. He hissed loudly, startling Musette.

"What on earth is going on?" Pillow snarled.

Musette, now fully awake, was almost glued to Pillow, unmoving and frozen with fear.

"I'll tell you what's going on," Vinnie informed. "You two and fat boy over there are on our island, and we don't like visitors."

"This is odd," Pillow replied. "We couldn't smell anyone's area. We would never invade another' s territory. We are English," he said proudly. "We are cats just like you."

"You're nothing like us. You wanna insult us, too, do you?" Spit hissed and began tapping Pillow around the head with his bent paw.

"Get off me," Pillow said, moving back.

"Enough, Spit," Vinnie ordered to calm things down. "You got two options. You can come nicely with us now, or you die. Those're your options. What's it gonna be?" He chewed on a piece of long hard, dry grass while waiting for Pillow to answer.

"Doesn't seem we have much choice, does it," Pillow said, glaring at Vinnie.

"I gave you two choices, didn't I?" Vinnie said as he winked at Musette.

"No, you gave us one!" Pillow spat, glaring at Vinnie with contempt.

"Hey, don't get smart with me. You think you're cleverer than me, do you?" Vinnie leaned toward Pillow, his face taut like a blank canvas and his left eye twitching. Vinnie's left eye always twitched when he was angry.

87

"Don't, Pillow," Musette pleaded. "Please don't say anything back to them, please don't."

"You should llisten to your Cattona, Pillow," Spit said. "Do as we say, and no one will get hurt."

"Right, then, love bugs. Let's go," ordered Mickey.

MEETING THE CATAQUERIANS

Danny and Tibby were talking. "So fat boy, you just sit around all day getting fed and only doing things when you want to? You're a bunch of Cattonas. No wonder you're so fat."

"Ummm," Tibby cleared his throat nervously. "Flattery will get you nowhere."

"Hey, stop using those fancy words. It ain't funny, do you hear me?"

"Yes," Tibby replied with a sigh.

Pillow, Tibby, and Musette followed Vernon and Spit, who led the way. Mickey smiled at Musette as she skipped shyly along, for he sensed she was feeling frightened and he didn't like to scare Cattonas. Vinnie, who was last in the line, was in deep thought. He wasn't quite sure what he was going to do with these unwelcome visitors when they all arrived back at the colony.

No one spoke. They just kept moving.

As they walked further away from the beach, Pillow, Tibby, and Musette saw they were entering an area surrounded by tall, sheltering trees. Paths began to appear, leading in many different directions. Finally, they had reached the colony.

Musette, Pillow, and Tibby saw Cattonas sitting in groups, chatting, tittering and giggling, while kittens ran about playing, or dangling tiny mice out of their mouths. There were mud huts with overhanging tropical vines providing plenty of shade, and more kittens were playfully pulling and twisting at long green vines as if they were string.

When Vinnie made a hissing sound, Vernon and Spit came to a stop in the middle of the colony, causing everyone behind them, except Vinnie, to fall like dominos.

"Is everyone okay?" Vernon asked.

Pillow, who was helping Musette up, and then Tibby, answered, "Yes, we're fine."

Vinnie, however, glared at Vernon. "I don't mean to interrupt you, Vernon, but can you remember these are intruders, not invited guests!"

Vernon shrugged and looked sheepish.

Everyone stood silently, looking at Vinnie and waiting to see what would happen next.

Vinnie, however, just stood and stared at the intruders. He realized he needed to know more, such as if there were more of them somewhere on the island. Feeling a little uneasy, Vinnie started circling the group, humming, *da da dee dee, da da dee dee,* as his tail lazily swished from side to side.

Musette looked at Pillow. "Is he okay?" she whispered.

But Spit answered with a laugh. "Not really. But then again, Vinnie's never okay."

Mickey turned to Musette. "He's just showing off. He does it all the time. Take no notice," he told her quietly.

The atmosphere began to feel friendlier as other Cataquerians began to appear, coming out of the mud huts. They gathered around, fascinated by the three new visitors with their red velvet collars.

Vinnie could see this was causing quite a stir. Since he loved to be noticed, he leapt into the air, spun like a top, and landed perfectly on all four paws. "Gather around, everyone! Gather around and get comfortable. Today when I was out hunting, I couldn't help but notice an unpleasant aroma coming up from the shore. Lo and behold, I discovered these three unwelcome visitors making themselves comfortable in our territory. And as the great leader and protector of our colony, I have taken them hostage for the protection of everyone here at Willows Rock!"

"You don't have to be scared of us," Pillow said. "We wouldn't hurt any of you. All we want is to be left alone in peace."

"I haven't finished," Vinnie warned in a twisted tone. "Don't ever interrupt me again."

"For heaven's sake," Musette huffed. "Who is this guy? Honestly, this is ridiculous."

The Cataquerians standing around nodded in agreement with Musette. They all knew the colony had plenty of food and supplies, and there was no reason to be concerned about three new cats.

Spit, who was next to Vinnie, noticed Vinnie was getting fed up. He now had his paws crossed over his chest.

"Spit, take the girl to Loops. I will deal with these two," Vinnie ordered.

"Who is Loops?" Musette asked nervously.

"I'm Loops." A little cat appeared from out of the crowd. Musette instantly sensed her sweet nature. "Please don't worry," Loops told Musette. "Come with me and you will be safe, I promise you."

"Well, if I must," Musette said, but she was reluctant to leave Pillow.

"Go on, Musette," Pillow told her gently. "We will be all right. I will talk to Vinnie. I am sure everything will be fine once he understands we are no threat to anyone here."

And so Musette followed Loops, but she turned around once more to look at Pillow.

He smiled back reassuringly and nodded his head as if to

tell her to leave. And then he turned back to face Vinnie as everyone else seemed to hold their breath.

GIRL TALK

"**C**ome in," Loops said. "This is our home."

Musette entered the little mud hut through a small door, immediately noticing how cozy and solid it felt. The floor was soft and comfortable, and there were different raised areas with bedding and food.

"Would you like a drink?" Loops asked.

"Please, I am so thirsty, thank you, that would be so kind of you," said Musette.

"Would you like milk, water, or juice?"

"Milk, please."

Loops poured out some milk for Musette. "Here you go. We always have plenty of milk to go around with so many mums on the island."

Musette drank a bit of milk, and then delicately wiped her mouth. She turned to Loops. "Why is your Catton keeping us here? That is, I presume you are a couple?"

"Yes, we are," Loops said proudly. Then she sighed deeply. "Vinnie does like to be in charge, but he won't harm you or your friends if you just do as he says."

"Do as he says?" Musette huffed. "It seems everyone does as he says, but what I can't understand is why? I mean, he doesn't seem the smartest or most attractive of all the Cattons here."

Loops's tail began to move back and forth for she felt protective of Vinnie. "He is our leader. And without him, we all would have been eaten by dogs by now, or scattered across the island like seashells, alone and without the protection of our colony."

"Oh Loops, I didn't mean to hurt your feelings," Musette said gently. "I can see you love Vinnie. But it can't be fun being around someone who is so angry all of the time."

"I do love him, I do. It's just that …" Loops hesitated.

"What?" Musette urged Loops to go on.

"It's just that I don't think he loves me," Loops said sadly.

"I don't think he could love anyone by the looks of him," Musette muttered.

Loops sat down and Musette sat next to her. "It's just that some days I feel like running away from here." And Loops began to pour her heart out to Musette.

They sat together for hours, talking and sharing their stories. Musette heard all about Loops and Vinnie, and life on Cataqueria Island. And Loops was fascinated with everything Musette told her about England, with its schools, people, houses, customs, and weather. Loops so wanted to travel and to live in a civilized way.

"I am so glad we met, Loops," said Musette. "We are going to be firm friends and I am going to make you see sense. I am going to change things around here!"

Vinnie was tired for it had been a long day. Spit had gone to get some coconut juice, and Vernon and Mickey had fallen asleep.

Pillow and Tibby were now lying down, feeling quite drained from the day's events. The other cats, no longer interested, were going about their business. Most had gone inside their huts while others just were relaxing and sipping from large shells.

Tibby sighed. "I don't understand any of this, do you, Pillow? It's all quite odd."

"I know, old boy," replied Pillow. "It's just silly. I mean how did that Vinnie get so much power over so many Cataquerians? It's not like he is—." Pillow stopped to consider if he should say what he thought out loud. But he did. "I wouldn't say he's particularly clever."

"Oh, he is not clever, Pillow, believe me, but he knows how to control others. I'll bet he is a nice chap once you get to know him. He is possibly just protecting his colony like he said," Tibby added.

"I wouldn't bet on it," Pillow said. "Did you notice how the other Cataquerians don't say anything back to him? He is nothing more than a bully. I mean just look at him over there, twittering with his partners in crime."

Pillow and Tibby could see Vinnie chatting to his henchcats. He was like a conductor orchestrating a small band. His paws were waving, his tail was swaying, and he looked like he was in his element.

In fact, Vinnie was trying to decide what to do about the intruders. He knew he had no option to but let them stay. Sending them away would be too easy, for they would surely settle elsewhere and what would be the fun in that?

Vinnie glanced over at Pillow and Tibby and began to move in their direction. But he would take a few paces, then stop and stand perfectly still. Then he would take a big breath before taking another step forward while tapping his nose in thought.

"What's he doing now?" Pillow wondered.

"Heaven knows," said Tibby. "It looks like some sort of dance, maybe the hokey cokey."

"Don't give me the giggles, Tibby," said Pillow. "Not now. We have to deal with this odd cat."

Finally, Vinnie appeared before Pillow and Tibby. "I have made my decision," he said. "I will allow you stay here at least until I get bored with you. There are a few empty huts at the end of the path," he said, pointing in that direction. "You can set up there."

"Thank you," said Pillow. "We are very grateful for your kindness."

"Yes," Tibby added, "it is most gracious of you to allow us to stay."

"Will you please let Musette know? Otherwise, she will be worried," said Pillow.

"Whatever, now just get out of my sight," Vinnie replied, sounding as tough as he possibly could.

SETTING UP HOME

Dogs weren't the only enemy on Cataqueria Island, for there were also rodents, wild boar, snakes, and monkeys, all of them a threat to young kittens. The Cattonas spent many hours clearing the earth, brushing away leaves, in fear of another enemy, the deadly scorpions, which sadly had killed a few Cataquerians.

Food was plentiful around Willows Rock but so were predators, so life was full of unpleasant surprises for both Cataquerians and their fellow Islanders. Security was paramount in the colony, and lessons on deadly predators were given to the kittens as soon as they could understand.

Vinnie strolled back to his hut where he found Musette and Loops chatting away.

"Hello, girls," he said with a smug smile. "Make yourself at home, lovely," he told Musette.

"Where are Pillow and Tibby?" she asked with wide eyes.

Your Catton and his sidekick? I gave them a hut each at the end of the colony. We don't want you next door, do we, ehhh? I mean you'd never leave me alone, would you?" Vinnie asked smugly.

"Oh, no," said Musette, rolling her eyes. "I mean we wouldn't want to love thy neighbor."

"What?" said Vinnie with a grin. "Did you say love so soon?" Then he sprawled out like a big flat black leaf. "Loops, get filing," he said, sticking out his paw in her direction.

Musette bit her lip in fear of saying something that might

provoke Vinnie. She decided, for Loops's sake, she must hold her tongue and leave gracefully.

"Yes, I had best go. Thank you so much, Loops, for your kind hospitality," Musette said, not mentioning Vinnie on purpose.

But he answered, "Anytime, sweet cheeks," and winked.

Loops walked Musette outside and stood with her near the hut. "I am so happy that you came here, Musette."

"Don't get so happy," Vinnie piped up from inside. "They won't be staying long. And hurry up, you have to finish my manicure."

Loops looked at Musette and hugged her tight. "I do hope to see you tomorrow. Perhaps we could have a milk together?"

"I would love nothing more," replied Musette.

"I will introduce you to all my friends. They are going to love you so much," said Loops.

"I can't wait," said Musette loudly. Then she whispered to Loops, "Is he always like this?"

"Yes," said Loops, "but he doesn't mean it. Honestly, he's not so bad."

"Hmm," Musette said. "I think I'm more shocked at how he speaks to you than I was when I fell into the ocean."

"LOOPS!" Vinnie now screeched, as loud as he could.

"Coming, Vinnie!" Loops said, and, throwing Musette a sad look, hurried back into the hut.

Musette stood for a moment, feeling as if she wanted to march back into the hut and give Vinnie a piece of her mind. But then she thought better of it, and turned to go, realizing, suddenly, that she had no idea where to go. Then she saw a female cat skipping towards her.

"Hi there!" the female said to Musette with a smile. "I'm Suzy Wong, Danny's sister.

Suzy Wong was tall and slender. She had two black patches

on each green eye. Her ears were yellow, and a wide white streak ran down the bridge of her nose and circled around her mouth. Her body was mixed with black and yellow fur. She was very pretty.

"Danny?" said Musette. "I don't think I've met him."

"Oh, you have. He found you today with Vinnie, I'm afraid to say."

"Oh no," sighed Musette, "not more trouble."

"Naaaaaah," said Suzy Wong. "We are a good family. We wouldn't want to hurt you or your Catton or the fat one. Is he your brother?"

"Brother?" Musette asked. "Goodness, do I look anything like him?"

"To be fair, no," said Suzy Wong, laughing. "But you never can tell, especially on this island. Follow me. I'll take you to the huts at the end of the colony that Vinnie has given you. It's very nice down there as you won't have many kittens near you, jumping in and out of your hut all day."

"Oh, but I'd love that," Musette said longingly.

"Haven't had any yet, I'm guessing?" asked Suzy Wong.

"No, and I never will. You see, I can't," said Musette.

Sensing Musette's sadness, Suzy Wong continued, "Well, there's plenty of kittens that need minding in the colony, and I'm sure the mums would be glad of a rest. "Oh, keep talking," Suzy Wong said suddenly.

"Why?" asked Musette.

"'Cos there's Mickey over there drinking with Vernon, my sister Suzy Wing's Catton."

Musette, who noticed how giddy Suzy Wong now was, looked over to see Mickey sitting in the shade outside Vernon's hut, chatting. Coconuts were piled outside and rats that had been skinned and boned were hanging and drying off long sticks. Mickey and Vernon saw Suzy Wong and Musette and waved.

"Hungry?" shouted Mickey. "Hold on," he told Vernon, and then raced over to the girls.

"Do you fancy taking a couple of rats with you?" Mickey asked.

"No," said Suzy Wong, "you can both stay where you are!" She laughed and Musette joined in.

"You're getting too cheeky, Suzy Wong," said Mickey, but he was grinning and didn't take his eyes off her. "What about you, Musette? Do you want some?"

"I would love some," she answered. "I don't fancy hunting this late."

"Hunting?" Suzy Wong asked, looking surprised. "You hunt?"

"You bet I do, and I'm better than the boys. I can catch anything that moves," Musette proudly announced.

"Wow! That is cool," Suzy Wong said. "But you can't do it here. It's forbidden."

"It might be forbidden here but not where I come from. And why is it forbidden here?" asked Musette.

"Because it is," said Suzy Wong. "Because we are needed here to do chores, cook, clean, and take care of the young."

The Cattonas wanted to hunt and explore the island on which they lived, but the Cattons wouldn't allow it. They – well, Vinnie mostly – wanted the Cattonas to tend to the young and not only cook for their Cattons, but to fix their sore paws when they returned home injured after a long day of hunting. The Cattons, led by Vinnie, were very chauvinistic!

"Oh, fishcakes!" muttered Musette, flapping her paws against her side.

"Well, my Cattona will never hunt," Mickey announced.

"But you don't have a Cattona," Suzy Wong said, hoping for a promising response.

"You're right, I don't," said Mickey teasingly. "So, three rats it is then . . . no, better make it four," he said, thinking of round Tibby. And he rushed back to the hut and snatched down four rats, then rushed back and gave them to Musette.

"Thank you, this is very nice," Musette said.

Mickey nodded and then turned to Suzy Wong. "Since you're going that way, why don't you come by for a drink after you drop Musette off?" Mickey grinned.

"Hmmm. Well, I may do, and I may not," Suzy Wong grinned right back.

Musette interrupted. "I had better hurry. Pillow will be worried about me."

"Okay," said Mickey. "I may see you tomorrow. And try not to worry. We aren't so bad."

"I gathered that," Musette smiled back at Mickey.

"Come on then, Musette," Suzy Wong said, "let's get you home."

When they reached the hut, Musette said goodbye to Suzy Wong, happy to have made another friend, and entered the hut. She ran right into Pillow's arms.

"Oh, Pillow, I am so glad to see you. I have so much to tell you," she said excitedly, dropping the rats on the floor.

"We were just about to come looking for you," Pillow said, motioning to Tibby who was standing nearby. "We were worried that Vinnie might keep you there."

"Oh, don't worry about him," Musette said.

"Look what we have done," Pillow said rather proudly, pointing to a pile of feathers neatly placed in the far corner above a ledge. And some coconut shells were lined up nearby to serve as water bowls.

Musette smiled. "How lovely."

Tibby now pointed to a screen of big palm leaves on one side of the hut. "And that's my bed, at least for tonight. I do like my privacy, as I'm sure you do as well. And tomorrow I will be moving into the hut next door. And what fine food you've brought," Tibby said.

"Yes, Mickey gave us these. And I met his future Cattona, Suzy Wong. Well, sort of. She hopes to be his Cattona at least. And tomorrow I am meeting Loops for milk. And then I may look after some kittens to just to help the other mums," Musette said with excitement and barely taking a breath.

"Okay, okay, calm down now," said Pillow, holding her tight. "I think we have some other things to discuss." *Like our future*, he thought. "For now, let's eat, sleep, and decide what we are going to do tomorrow. Remember, we are just guests here."

"I know." sighed Musette. "But I just know whatever happens, it will be okay."

As Pillow cuddled Musette, his eyes caught Tibby's, and the two of them shared a look of uncertainty that Musette didn't see.

WILLOWS CIRCLE

In the morning, all three cats woke up bright, rested, and glad of the hut, which was certainly comfortable and already felt like home. Musette was preening herself, purring next to Pillow when suddenly Loops was outside calling her. Musette leapt up and ran outside, leaving Pillow yawning and rubbing his paws over his eyes.

The day was just waking up and everything felt cool and fresh. Lovely scents of flowers and fruit filled the air as if the ocean breeze had reached the colony, bringing with it a spray of perfume.

"Good morning, sunshine," Musette greeted Loops, smiling.

"Good morning. Did you sleep well?" Loops asked.

"Yes, it was very cozy and more than adequate. I feel ready for the day."

"Come on, then," Loops said. "Let's go down to the main circle. That's the centre of our colony where Vinnie took you yesterday. There, I will introduce you to some of the other Cattonas. We can have our milk there, too. Have you eaten yet?"

"Not yet," said Musette. "I'm fine, though I might catch something later."

Loops gasped. "You hunt?"

"Yes, I was telling Suzy Wong this yesterday evening. I hunt and I intend to keep hunting while I am here."

"You met Suzy Wong then?"

"Yes, she is very nice."

Loops giggled. "She likes Mickey."

"Oh, I know," Musette added. "If Suzy Wong has her way, there will be a wedding soon."   "Did you meet Suzy Wing, her twin? She is married to Vernon, and she's okay but very different from her sister, nice but in a different sort of way." And off went Loops and Musette, chatting away like they had been friends for years.

A little later, Tibby and Pillow decided to go for a stroll to look around. They also hoped they would be able to talk to some of the Cataquerians about the colony and the island.

They walked along the winding paths and past various huts. Everyone seemed friendly and waved their paws at Tibby and Pillow. When they reached the centre of the colony, they spotted Musette chatting with other Cattonas. She looked happy and content and was holding a few kittens in her arms. She didn't even notice Tibby and Pillow.

Spit was sitting by a long ledge, arms stretched out on either side, gazing up at the sun and thinking about what he could do that day.

"Let's go and talk to him," Tibby told Pillow, and they strolled over to Spit.

"Hi, there," said Pillow. Do you mind if we join you?"

Spit looked around to see if Vinnie was in sight. "I don't know. We aren't supposed to be friends. I'm one of Vinnie's and I don't want no trouble, at least not from him."

"Oh, we don't either," said Tibby reassuringly. "We just want to know what's on this island and how the heck can we get off it."

"Charming," Spit hissed. "Talk that way and I'll be taking you off it myself." Spit was easily agitated. He could be wound up like a clockwork mouse, especially by Vinnie, who knew how to get Spit going.

"I meant no harm, it's just my sense of humor," said Tibby. "We are so very grateful for your kind hospitality. Honestly, we are."

This seemed to calm Spit down a bit, so Pillow now asked, "So, are there any other colonies on the island?"

"Yeah, a few," Spit said. "Small ones though. But on the other side of the island, about a day's walk away, there are Doggeroes up at Bellows Edge, near Diggets Cave."

"Really?" Pillow asked, shooting a look at Tibby.

"Yes, but we never seem them. We didn't get on with them, so Vinnie made them leave and now they keep to themselves, thank goodness. They're a right bunch of savages; they killed many of us. Don't go wandering up there, 'cos you'll never come back," Spit warned.

"Oh, we won't," said Tibby feeling fearful. "Do pray tell us where they are exactly."

"Okay, you see up there at the highest point?" Spit was standing up, pointing to the mountain, which was about three miles inland. "Just up there, where the fresh water comes down. If you go beyond the waterfall, you're bound to meet one and they will crush you with their big teeth in seconds."

"Oh, whiskers," said Pillow, "that's not good. It must be hard not being able to roam where you want to given you're living so near to danger."

"Well, we really never go there, and they don't come here, 'cos of Vinnie."

"What do you mean?" Pillow asked.

"I mean that they're scared of Vinnie. He could easily blind them, if not kill 'em. That's our Vinnie," Spit said proudly.

Just then Vernon arrived with Suzy Wing, who did look exactly like her twin sister, Suzy Wong.

Tibby, Pillow, and Spit all said hello at the same time.

"See you later," Suzy Wing said with a wave of her paw. "I will go and chat with the girls."

"Snap!" shouted Tibby, which made all cats look at him as if he was crazy. "It's just a game." Tibby shrugged.

"Game?" said Vernon, raising his voice. "It's a game having you three new cats here. Vinnie loves a good game, don't he?" he said, as Spit laughed.

"Well, it's not a game to us," said Pillow. "We just want to know what to do. We are not seeking to upset anyone and just want to know if we can stay in peace for a while, at least until we find a way off the island."

"Off the island?" screamed Vinnie, as he walked towards them. "I will tell you when you can get off the island."

All the cats turned around to look at him since they hadn't heard him coming. Vinnie could often be very sneaky, creeping up when you least expected him.

"Oh, I didn't mean it like that, Vinnie," Pillow said sincerely. "I think this is a wonderful island and colony, and I thank you again for having us, but as I was saying to your friends—"

"They ain't friends," interrupted Vinnie. "They're like brothers to me, blood brothers. Do you understand what that means?

"Yes," said Pillow. "You're all very close."

"Ha! 'Close'? No, it means we like blood," Vinnie said with a sneer.

"Well, anyway, as I was saying," Pillow said, then stopped to think for a second. "We just want to go home, or if that's not possible, then just settle as best as we can."

"Oh, so now you want to go home!" screamed Vinnie. "Ain't we good enough for you?!"

By now a crowd was gathering, which is what Vinnie loved. An audience.

Tibby interrupted. "Vinnie, must you make everything an argument? I mean, really, it is most upsetting."

Vinnie stepped back, away from Pillow and glared at Tibby. "Who's arguing here, me or you, ehh, fat cat? And besides, who threw you a fish?"

"No one." Tibby replied, "no one, Vinnie. Come on, Pillow, let's go back to the hut."

"Oi, fat cat, did I say you could go?" Vinnie yelled.

"Now look," said Pillow. "I am a fair and decent chap, Vinnie, and I wish you or your friends, brothers, fellow Cattons —"

"Oh, get on with it," grumbled Vinnie.

"No harm, but I need to know how long we can stay here. We don't want any trouble form you or your colleagues," Pillow said, quite reasonably.

Vinnie sat down, perfectly still, rubbing his paw under his chin. "How long can you stay here? Let me think. Well, how long do you want to stay here?" he asked nicely, smiling at Pillow.

"I'm not sure yet," Pillow replied.

"Well, nor am I!" Vinnie yelled, and he leapt away into the bushes.

The days were flying by and Pillow and Tibby started coming to Willows Circle each morning, often spending hours just chatting with the Cataquerians. Tibby had even started a journal that relayed forthcoming news and featured a calendar. And Musette spent a lot of time helping Cattonas care for their kittens.

Vinnie was watching them all with fascination. He could see they were gaining respect amongst the colony and was beginning to feel threatened by their presence.

Musette had also set up a play school for the kittens in one of the empty huts near the circle. She had filled it with long vines, sticks, and pebbles so the kittens could play and learn to count. She brought in food for the kittens' snacks, such as small fish she caught in the lagoon. She had also organized a milk morning for the young mums to meet while some of the single females watched the kittens. Musette chatted with all the Cattonas about life in England and how everyone looked out for each other. She told stories of how the English cats often lived in harmony with Doggeroes.

The female Cataquerians felt so empowered by Musette. They admired her strength and the way she behaved around Pillow, as his equal. They loved how Pillow showed nothing but respect for his Cattona. Musette was also confident around the Cattons and didn't respond to their silly jokes or teasing. Musette's personality was rubbing off on the other Cattonas, especially Loops who so wanted Vinnie to treat her the way Pillow loved and treated Musette.

By the time the three English cats had been on Cataqueria Island for six weeks, they were far too busy to miss their old life. Although things were very different on the island, Tibby, Pillow, and Musette were beginning to feel very settled. They did think about Mr. and Mrs. Supreme, but they began to feel as if they were living a life that somehow was meant to be. After all, they were animals that had no choice but to be as they were designed to be.

Pillow decided the best way to get along with Vinnie was to flatter his ego and try to befriend him. Pillow also understood that it was unlikely he, Musette, and Tibby would be rescued anytime soon, so they all had no option but to try and get along.

THE VOTE

One-night Vinnie called out, "Loops! Sharpen my claws!" Then he took a seat in front of the other Cataquerians who were gathered in the center of the colony, talking together quietly after the dinner hour. Musette, Pillow, and Tibby were there, too.

Loops began to tend to Vinnie's paws. She was quiet, but Musette, who was horrified by this display of Vinnie's power over Loops, was not.

"I've had enough of this," Musette said, and walked off in disgust. A few other Cattonas followed Musette, although from their expressions, they seemed a bit nervous.

Pillow called after Musette, joking, "Musette, that's how to treat your Catton." But Musette didn't turn around. She was not amused.

Nor was Vinnie. "Ha ha," he said, "but I do the jokes around here, Monkey Boy."

"It was just a joke," Pillow told Tibby, ignoring Vinnie as he so often did.

"Don't fret, Musette's probably just tired. But I do like this island life, Pillow, I must say," Tibby added. "It's very in favor of us guys, and maybe that's not such a bad way, Pillow."

"I'm not sure about that, but I do want to know what Vinnie's up to." Pillow almost whispered to Tibby so that Vinnie couldn't hear. "I believe Spit, Vernon, and Mickey are all a bit simple. They believe Vinnie's tall tales, but I don't. And I don't understand him. First, he tells us we can stay, and then he gets angry when the other cats in the colony try to befriend us."

He seems such a cold character. I wonder why he feels the way he does. Why he is so bitter about life? thought Pillow.

Vinnie did not seem to have feelings for anyone or anything and was always angry. But what Pillow didn't know was that Vinnie's mother had rejected him after he was born, believing the tiny black kitten was too weak to live very long. He couldn't feed as well as his siblings, and had 27 claws, and small, slit-like eyes that looked like buttonholes. So, like all her ancestors had done before her, she had left the weakest kitten in the litter alone to die in order to give her other kittens a better chance at survival. And one day, she kissed Vinnie goodbye, licked his eyes, gathered up her other kittens, and went off to build a new nest.

Vinnie slept for three days and then woke up hungry, thirsty, and very weak. He somehow found the strength to crawl to a coconut that had fallen from a tree and cracked open. With his little claws, which were as sharp as pins, he scraped out some coconut flesh to eat. From that day on, he got stronger and stronger. But Vinnie never forgot the loneliness and desperation he felt as a kitten.

As he grew up, Vinnie wandered around the island until he eventually found the other cats. He hung around their homes, meowing, and hoping someone kind would hear his cries. One day a couple of old island cats took pity on him and dragged him into their home. They offered him shelter and food on the condition that once he was old enough to hunt, he would provide food for all three of them. And the old cats also told him they didn't care if he stayed or left, which meant they didn't care about him. This was the old Cataquerian way. But they told Vinnie that if he did leave, the island dogs would surely eat him.

So Vinnie grew up hunting, most days providing food for the ungrateful old fat cats who never showed him any love. In Vinnie's mind, however, they were his family, and he was grateful for the warm nest, clean water, and company they gave him.

Despite his difficult start in life, Vinnie grew up strong, making friends easily and influencing others. He had a charm about him, and no other cat on the island ever had 27 claws. Slowly, Vinnie became a leader, and slowly he won over delicate little Loops, whom he loved as much as he could love anyone. But Vinnie still had an empty space inside.

Vernon was sitting with Spit, talking about the great big catfish he had caught earlier that day, when they both saw Vinnie coming toward them. He had kept the spikes he'd removed from the catfish since he liked keeping items that could hurt.

"Hey, Vinnie, the man. What's up?" Vernon asked when he saw Vinnie.

"Keep it down," Vinnie whispered. "Listen, I've decided we need to do something to get rid of Pillow and Tibby. Don't worry about noisy one, she can stay," he added, nudging Spit.

Spit laughed. "She would eat you up and spit you out, Vinnie."

Vinnie looked at Spit in surprise. "Me? Are you saying I couldn't handle that little Cattona?"

Spit shrugged, not wanting to make Vinnie mad.

"And besides," said Vinnie, "I've had enough of them. My Loops is acting strange. She's not filing my claws right. And the Kit and Mixes are smiling more at that wishy-washy bore than at me. I'm telling you, they've got to go."

"Oh, take no notice," Vernon said. "They're okay really. I haven't seen any screeching, annoying kittens in a while, and surely that's a blessing."

"NO!" shouted Vinnie. "That's because The Mouth has put them all in huts everyday like a mad Cattona, teaching them this and that. It's crazy, some of the nonsense she feeds into their little minds!"

"I don't know. They look happy enough to me and I know my lot are sure sleeping better," Vernon added.

"Oh, do be quiet, Vernon. I do believe you're getting brainwashed by those do-gooders! I want them gone or else! Do you want me gone? Because I will leave this colony high and dry if this disloyalty continues, do you hear me? And as soon as I've gone, those Doggeroes will come down here and have you all for dinner! I want those two Cattons gone, and soon, or there will be trouble! So let's play their game," Vinnie said.

"What do you mean?" Vernon asked, unsure what Vinnie was up to.

"I mean, we'll hold a meeting and ask everyone to vote on whether to allow those nitwits to stay. Vernon, you'll collect the votes while Spit and I keep everyone else busy."

"But I can't count," muttered Vernon.

"You nitwit! That's the reason why I am asking you to do it!" Vinnie yelled.

Vernon looked puzzled.

"We collect the leaves, red leaves will mean 'out,' and green leaves will mean they can stay. Then you just come back after counting the votes with more red leaves than green ones. It's simple, Vernon. Even you can do that, can't you?" Vinnie asked.

"Oh, so I don't even have to count them because they all look the same?" Vernon asked, still not sure about this.

"No," Vinnie said, getting angrier by the second. "Some are red and some are green!"

"Yeah, but they're all still leaves," Vernon said, "so they look the same."

Vinnie sighed, and then asked slowly, "Do you understand what we are going to do?"

Vernon thought very hard for a moment and then finally said, "Yeah, I got it, boss. We end up with more red than green, right?"

"Yes!" Vinnie said with a huff. "I will bring them down a peg or two, especially that Pillow who thinks he is more popular than me. He'll be in for a shock when he sees he isn't so liked."

Spit had been listening carefully. "I like it, Vinnie. I like it a lot. I'll go tell the others that we are having a meeting tonight. In fact, I'll tell them to bring some food and drink. We haven't had a gathering for quite a while. It could be a fun night."

"Sure, why not?" Vinnie said. "Let's show them what style is. Who knows, I may even get a little smile out of Musette. I know she likes me."

"She likes you all right!" Spit rolled his eyes.

But Vinnie didn't even notice. "It's my charm. You see, Spit, some of us have it and some of us don't . . . and you don't!"

Pillow and Musette had spent the day at Willows Circle with most of the Cataquerians. Even Spit, Mick, and Danny were enjoying their company and hearing how life used to be. They even agreed it could do no harm to let the Cattonas hunt. In fact, this would give them time to do other things, like laze around in the sun and spend more time with their kittens.

Musette had taken some of her friends down to the shore where they all splashed about catching ray fish. It was an amazing day and the girls felt so liberated and happy to be contributing food for their families, while the Cattons were glad of the peace.

But when Pillow, Musette, and Tibby heard there was going to be a meeting that night, they felt a little apprehensive.

"I wonder what Vinnie's going to say," Tibby wondered.

"I doubt anything nice," said Musette.

"Oh, let's not think the worst," Pillow said. "He could be just having one of his usual turns. According to Vernon, Vinnie just likes talking out loud."

"Yes, he just loves an audience, whoever it is," Musette agreed, and shook her head.

Back in their hut, Vinnie had an audience of one – Loops – and was telling her, "So, my little love nest, you know I am not happy with things here since your friends have arrived. I expect some loyalty from you," he said in a persuasive tone.

"I am always loyal to you, Vinnie," said Loops. "But I am so much happier now Musette is here, and I think she, Pillow and Tibby have been good for us all. They do like you so very much."

"I'm not here to be liked!" snapped Vinnie. "And stop all this silly admiration of those three. I find it very annoying."

"I am sorry, Vinnie, but I am not going to stop being friends with them because you don't like them."

"My, my," said Vinnie, "we are getting brave these days. Do you want me to leave you all alone? I can easily leave you, Loops. Why, there are plenty who could take your place," he said calmly. "I mean admittedly you're good with a flint but you ain't all that."

Loop stared at Vinnie. "Go ahead, do your worst," she said as her tailed swayed. "And you'll see who is lonely then. I'm a good Cattona, Vinnie, but I want more out of this relationship than filing claws and washing bowls."

"Ha ha ha ha!" he laughed. "That firecracker has really got to you, hasn't she? Well listen to me, little Miss Easily Led, I make the decisions around here and no one else. So, watch and learn, watch and learn. Let's go," Vinnie said. "It's time to shine, it's my time to shine."

Loops sighed, following him outside and shaking her head. *What next?* she thought.

When they arrived at Willows Circle, nearly all the Cataquerians were sitting around. Pillow, Musette, and Tibby were chatting with a nice family who thanked them for the peaceful mornings since their kittens were so well behaved these days.

Vinnie took his position, leaping onto a tall platform in front of everyone, and Loops stood off to his side.

"This will be good," Musette said to Pillow. She looked up at Loops and winked at her. Loops rolled her eyes up as if to say, "I don't know about this."

"Quiet!" shouted Vinnie. "Can I have your attention?!"

Everyone stopped talking and looked toward Vinnie, which seemed to make him puff up.

"Now," he said, thinking as he spoke, "as you know, we have welcomed and entertained our three guests," he said, pointing in Musette, Pillow, and Tibby's direction.

"Didn't see that coming," Musette whispered to Pillow.

Vinnie stared at Musette and continued. "And I have done my best to welcome them since they arrived here . . ."

"Seven weeks ago!" shouted a young male cat proudly, since he had, thanks to Musette, just learnt how to count days.

"Ahhh, said Vinnie sadly, "you're a fine example of what troubles me. Counting days, how sad!" he screeched as the young male cat cowered.

"Counting days, counting mice, counting coconuts, counting this, counting that!" Vinnie continued, growing more frenzied. "Count my claws! Oh yes, count them! They are the only things any of you should be counting around here," and he waved his paw in the air, pointing at everyone around him. "What is happening? We were once happy with our lives! There was no counting, but there were rules! And now? Now Cattonas are out fishing and hunting while their kittens are locked up in the morning, kept inside counting pebbles! And we have our fat cat local gossip writing down everything for all to see and twisting everything around!"

Tibby looked horrified, but Pillow warned him quietly, "Say nothing."

Vinnie continued. "You are all turning into nothing more than a pack of ants marching around our colony," he said with his paws above his head impersonating a big ant marching up and down. "Ants, ants, we are ants!"

Suddenly Vinnie stopped and stood quite still. Everyone was silent.

"But, I, as your leader and protector, have decided enough is enough! I will give you all the opportunity to decide if this way of life is your way of life or if you want to live as you lived before on this island as good, decent Cattons and Cattonas. I will allow you, my Cataquerians, to decide because I am a fair leader. I believe we all have the right to choose good or bad," Vinnie said, staring right at Pillow.

"Here, here!" shouted Spit, trying to rile Vinnie.

Vernon jumped in, too. "Yeah, go on, Vinnie!" He and Spit were sniggering.

Vinnie, feeling full of himself, continued. "The decision is yours!" And with that he leapt off his stage and ran through the crowd, swishing and slicing his claws above everyone's heads, hoping to scare their tails off.

Loops ran over to Musette. "I am so sorry," she said. "Vinnie is feeling insecure."

"Don't worry, Loops," reassured Musette. "He is just a foolish Catton. He proved that with his silly speech."

"He just doesn't get it," added Pillow. "Sometimes change is scary."

"Yes, I think you are probably right," said Loops kindly.

"At least he is giving everyone the opportunity to vote," said Tibby. "I never thought Vinnie was the democratic type, but he never ceases to amaze me."

"Nor me," said Loops. "See you tomorrow, then."

"Yes, good night," said the three cats and they headed home.

Vinnie paced nervously up and down in his hut, hoping he had sown the seed of doubt into the other Cataquerians. After about ten minutes, he strolled back to Willows Circle to see if there was a change in the atmosphere now that he had made his thoughts clear to the colony. As he walked, he thought, *I will finally get rid of that stupid, dull, wishy-washy bore who has no respect for me, no respect whatsoever! As for his Cattona, she's pretty enough but ain't she got a mouth on her, telling him what to do all the time, and he gets up and does it! He's short of a coconut or two, or maybe he's just scared of her!*

In the Circle, Vinnie found himself alone, for there was now no one about. He couldn't sense anything in the atmosphere and began suddenly to doubt things. He chewed on one of his claws and his mind spun. Then he had an idea.

Later, Pillow and Musette were outside of their hut. No one was saying much, for all were a bit tired after the day and Vinnie's big announcement about the vote. Pillow had caught a large bird for dinner, and Tibby was now readying the fire on which to roast it, while Musette was plucking its feathers. Then she looked up.

"Oh, no, now what?" she muttered. "Here comes Mr. Happy."

Vinnie was marching towards.

"Oh, dear," said Tibby. "What's wrong now?'

"Why, good afternoon, Pillow," Vinnie said, ignoring the other two. "May I speak with you privately?"

Pillow cast a look at Musette and Tibby, and then moved over to Vinnie. "Yes, Vinnie?"

"Well, here's what I have been thinking," Vinnie said. "I have decided to spare you some embarrassment and ask you to quietly leave the colony on your own. You can head to the other side of the island where the other misfits live. You'll fit in better there."

"But, Vinnie, we like being here. It's a wonderful colony. I don't think it would be fair if we left now since we have made so many friends. And what about Loops and Musette? They would miss each other so much. How could you tell Loops that you made us leave?"

"Oh, you'd love that, wouldn't you, a big drama in front of Loops, making me look like the bad one." Vinnie asked.

"No I wouldn't, I wouldn't at all, but I have my Cattona and Tibby to think about, and you have your Cattona who dearly loves you but doesn't deserve to lose her best friend."

Vinnie's mind spun. His plan wasn't quite working. He also realized it might be risky to make Pillow leave, particularly since he could take half the colony with him, even Loops.

"Okay," Vinnie said, "I tried to give you a graceful way out, but we'll have the vote. I will let the Cataquerians decide. That's better than just killing you, isn't it, because you know I could."

"Oh, for heaven's sake," Musette piped up. "Who on earth

118

do you think you're talking to, Vinnie? You might have a few extra toes but that's about it."

Vinnie started jumping up and down, paws clenched and his ears so far back that they looked like they had vanished. He was so mad his eyes were glazed over. "I will feed you all to a giant lizard like buzzing, annoying flies, because that's all you are to me! Flies that get in the way!"

"Vinnie, it doesn't have to be like this," said Pillow calmly. "We could be friends. I mean that, Vinnie. You have so many qualities I don't have."

At this Vinnie stopped, composed himself, licked his paw and brushed it through the fur on his head. "Well, at least we agree on something. Go on, tell me more," he said.

As Musette and Tibby looked at Pillow, he tried to think what he could say about Vinnie that was halfway decent. "Well, you can slice a coconut in seconds. You walk like no other cat on this Island . . ."

"Stop!" shouted Vinnie holding his paw out straight. "Listen, Monkey Boy, I don't want you as my friend. I don't even like you, so get that out of your head." And he walked away slowly with his head high and tail moving very slowly to show he never needed to run.

And as Vinnie swaggered away, Tibby, Pillow, and Musette stood quietly together, watching him, each lost in their own thoughts about not only Vinnie, but about what might happen to them next.

IN OR OUT

Musette was up bright and early. She was meeting the mums for milk. She didn't feel relaxed or happy for she had heard from Suzy Wing that the vote was being organized today.

As she arrived at Willows Circle, she sat down with Loops and Suzy Wong and decided to raise her concerns about the vote with them.

"What if we don't win the vote," Musette said fearfully. "I mean we don't talk to everyone and who knows what Vinnie has said to them."

"I honestly don't know why your worrying, Musette," said Suzy Wong kindly. "I really believe that you will win this paws down. I don't know any Cataquerian that doesn't want you, Pillow, or Tibby here."

"Then why is Vinnie holding this vote?" Musette asked. "If he knows we are going to win, what's the point of it all?"

"I love Vinnie," Loops said, "but I don't trust him. He is being too fair about this."

"I know what Vinnie's up to," said Suzy Wing, who now joined the group.

"What?" asked Loops.

"He has asked Vernon to fix the vote, counting more 'out's' than 'in's'," Suzy Wing said.

"I knew it!" Musette had jumped up and flapped her paws together.

"Shhhh, Musette," said Loops gently. "If Vinnie finds out

we know this, he will be angry with Vernon. Vinnie hates disloyalty more than anything."

"Yes, and Vernon would be angry with me, too," said Suzy Wing.

"Okay, our lips are sealed, but what are we going to do?" Musette asked. "Pillow or Tibby won't stay if the vote is 'out'. I know Pillow would never go against democracy."

"Yes, and Vinnie knows that," said Loops.

"We can't let this happen. We Cattonas need to fix this," Suzy Wing said.

"How? And what am I going to say to Pillow?" Musette wondered.

"Let's regroup later to discuss our plans," Suzy Wing added. "And in the meantime, everyone get thinking. We are running out of time."

Meanwhile, Pillow and Tibby were sitting outside their hut wondering about their future.

"It is apparent we are well liked here," Tibby said. "And according to my feedback from most of the Cataquerians I know, the vote should go overwhelmingly in our favor. So, what is the point of it all?"

"I guess it's just another opportunity for Vinnie to get up and prance around, waving his paws and stamping his feet," sighed Pillow. "But I take nothing for granted. You just never know," he added, looking concerned.

Vinnie was skipping about Willows Circle, flicking his claws in, and out singing "Love is tough when it ain't enough. Dee daa dee daa." He was feeling very confident about his plan. He couldn't wait to stand up and reveal the vote in front of all the Cataquerians and finally tell Pillow that he was leaving and wasn't as popular as he thought. *I will show him*, Vinnie thought and beamed.

Down on the beach, Mickey, Spit, Vernon, and Danny were chatting. They agreed that Pillow, Musette, and Tibby were decent enough and were good for the colony, but the four Cattons were still loyal to Vinnie.

Back at Willows Rock, the girls had just finished discussing their plan.

"So, does everyone understand what is going to happen?" said Musette.

"Yes. Vinnie isn't going to be happy," Loops said, "but I will deal with him. He can't have it all his way. When the vote goes in favor of you staying, he won't go back on his word, even if it kills him. He is funny like that."

"Oh well, perhaps he does have some good qualities after all," said Musette.

"He does," said Loops. "He just doesn't know it.

At day's end, Spit and Vernon were busy collecting the votes, going from hut to hut. The Cataquerians would place either a green ("in") or red ("out") leaf into coconut shells. Spit collected the green leaves while Vernon collected the red. As they gathered up the leaves, it became apparent how much the newcomers were liked. Spit's coconut shell was already filled with green leaves, while Vernon had collected only one red leaf.

"Flying monkeys," said Vernon. "This ain't going well at all. Vinnie isn't going to be happy."

"Nah," said Spit, "but he'll be happy when he fixes the vote. Pillow and his crew can go do good somewhere else. They'll be okay wherever they go. They're a smart bunch, that's for sure."

And Vernon and Spit continued collecting votes, feeling a bit guilty about all this.

When they were done, they met with Vinnie who asked about the result.

"Well, Vinnie," Spit said, "they got one red vote to leave and the rest to stay.

Vinnie's eye narrowed for a second. "Who wanted them out? Was it a secret admirer of mine?" Vinnie now looked smug. "She clearly has good taste."

Spit couldn't help himself and burst out laughing. "Good taste? It was an old Cataquerian who can't see or hear a thing!"

Vinnie brushed off the remark, pretending he hadn't heard, but he began to pace and think. *I'll bet that bossy boots of Pillow's got all the Cattonas to vote to let them stay.* He stopped pacing and turned to Vernon. "Take the leaves, pretend to count them, and bring the results to me once I am on my ledge."

"O-k-kay," Vernon stuttered. "But I don't feel too comfortable going on the ledge in front of everyone. I'm sh-shy."

"*WHAT?!*" screeched Vinnie. "Shy? You weren't shy when you were banging on hut doors! Just get a grip and do as I say!"

Spit now spoke up. "I hope this is going to work, Vinnie . . ."

"Oh, shut up, Spit. When there's a vote, I always win. And when everyone gathers, we will announce it."

Pillow and Musette finished their supper and were getting ready to head down to Willow Circle with the other Cataquerians.

"I do hope things go in our favor," said Tibby. "I like living here."

"Me, too," said Musette, "although I do miss Mrs. Supreme. I wonder how she is."

"I bet she is doing fine," said Pillow. "And she will know we are safe. She was very knowing."

"Yes, it's called a sixth sense. You feel things in your gut," said Tibby.

"So, what do you feel in yours?" Musette asked. "Do you think we will be staying or leaving?"

"The only thing I'm feeling is wind," Tibby said, rubbing his stomach.

Musette laughed. "Well, come along then, it's time and the walk to Willows Circle may help your tummy." And off they went.

When they reached Willows Circle, they mingled with the other Cataquerians who had gathered. Musette joined the Wong twins while Pillow and Tibby were greeted by Twinkles. At thirteen she had grey skin and little fur, with spikes of hair coming out of her small pink ears, which Tibby found rather attractive. Twinkles was very delicate and highly intelligent.

"Hello, young man," she said. "Feeling optimistic I hope?"

"Well, who knows," Tibby said, feeling a bit bashful. "With Vinnie it could go either way."

"Yes," Twinkles said, "but he can't go against the colony. Even he is not that stupid. And look how well Musette and Loops get along. Surely, he wouldn't want to spoil their friendship."

"I wouldn't bet on that," said Pillow, "but whatever happens, we will respect the vote."

Musette saw Twinkles talking to Tibby and smiled. Then Suzy Wong said, "Let's stay here close to the ledge. That way we will get a good view of Vinnie."

"Fine by me," said Musette.

Suddenly Vinnie leapt onto the ledge. Spit, Vernon, Mickey, and Danny stood nearby, but all kept their eyes on the ground. They couldn't look into the eyes of their fellow Cataquerians in fear that they would see their shame.

Vinnie now jumped up and down and spun around,

shaking his head to wake himself up. He landed on his front paws, hind legs in the air, and stood in a handstand for a few seconds.

"What on earth is he doing?" said Musette.

"Trying to look important," Suzy Wong said.

"It looks like he's talking from his rump!" said Suzy Wing.

Vinnie suddenly jumped back onto all four paws and smiled at the crowd. "Dear fellow Cataquerians, the results of the vote are in. I am hoping it will be in the favor of our dear friends," he said, casting a sly look at Pillow. "Vernon, bring me the votes. Do hurry. The suspense is killing me!" he said and burst out laughing.

Vernon slowly walked over to Vinnie, holding the two coconut shells in his hands. One was full to the top with red leaves and the other appeared empty.

The crowd went silent with disbelief as Pillow lowered his head.

Tibby put his paw on his Pillow's shoulder. "Don't worry, old friend. We knew we couldn't stay forever."

As muttering began in the crowd, Suzy Wing leaned over to her kitten, Sunny, and whispered in his ear. He took off, racing through the crowd like a flash of lighting.

Vinnie continued. "It seems you have voted for our friends to leave the colony. This comes as no surprise to me since I warned you all of their foolish ways. But do feast and enjoy the evening!" he said, obviously quite pleased with events. Vinnie was just about to leap off of the ledge when Sunny came running back through the crowd, which parted for him as he headed straight to his mother.

"*JUST A MINUTE!*" Suzy Wing now yelled and held up an armful of green leaves. "Vernon dropped these outside our hut. They need to be added to the vote."

Vernon looked a little confused, but Sunny proudly shouted, "I found them! I went and got them for you, Dad!"

"Shut up, you fool!" snapped Vinnie, who then glared at Vernon. "You're as stupid as your father!"

Loops now shouted back to Vinnie, "He is not stupid. Don't speak about a kitten like that."

There was a hush in the crowd as everyone looked from Loops to Vinnie, wondering what he might do. Musette took hold of Loops's paw and held it tightly. But now Vernon, feeling a surge of anger, spoke up, too. "Don't call my son stupid, Vinnie."

Vinnie's claws snapped out and he arched his back. "How dare you answer me back, you dimwit. Your son is a liar!"

But Vernon's claws were now out, and his tail was banging the floor like a hammer hitting a nail. "My son ain't no liar, Vinnie."

Sunny started to cry as Suzy Wing grabbed him and held him tight.

"I only did what you asked me, mummy," he said, as Suzy Wong shushed him.

Suzy Wong, fearing Vinnie would hear, now shouted, "Mickey, I will *NEVER* cross paws with you if you don't stand by my sister and Vernon and tell the truth. Let everyone know what Vinnie was up to!"

Mickey, knowing he loved Suzy Wong too much to lose her, walked slowly over to Vinnie. "Listen, Sunny is a good kid. Don't do this, Vinnie. And don't hurt Vernon. He's done nothing wrong."

Vinnie started twitching all over. He couldn't lose face in front of his colony.

"Listen, Vinnie," Mickey whispered, "you can turn this around. You need to do the right thing here. If you don't, we'll have big problems in the colony."

But Vinnie fumed. He pointed at Vernon. "You're no blood brother! No privileges for you! You're just like all the other Cataquerians from now on!"

Vernon saw Suzy Wing smiling at him, and he could feel her heart bursting with pride. He suddenly felt more of a Catton than ever before. "That's fine with me, Vinnie," Vernon said, and moved over to stand with his Cattona and Sunny.

Pillow whispered to Musette, "Poor Vernon, but at least Sunny found those leaves."

"Oh, he did indeed. After I put them there," Musette said.

Pillow looked at Musette in shock. "You did *WHAT*!?"

"I will explain it all later, Pillow."

Mickey nudged Vinnie again, and after a moment of silence, he sighed and spoke. "There seems to have been an error in the voting because some leaves were lost, and then found." He glared at Sunny, but Mickey nudged Vinnie again.

"Wind it up, Vinnie, before you lose more than just this vote," Mickey whispered.

But suddenly Pillow stepped forward and climbed onto the ledge. "I would like to say something if I may."

"Oh, for rotten rats," grumbled Vinnie, but Mickey pulled him back and gave Pillow the stage.

"Without this vote we would never have felt comfortable here. And thanks to Vinnie, who's right for democracy, he and all of you have made us bona fide residents of Cataquerian Island. On behalf of Musette, Tibby, and myself, I would like to thank each and every one of you, but especially Vinnie and of course Vernon for all his hard work today. So, on the count of three, *HIP, HIP, HOORAY!*"

And the crowd joined in with Pillow, hip-hip-hooraying, and pointing their raised paws in Vinnie's direction, praising him.

127

Vinnie now shined like the moon and stood tall, basking in the glory and waving his paws around his head as if he had just finished winning a big race. "Thank you, thank you!" he said in a dreamy state. Then he leaned over to Pillow and whispered, "Get down before I push you off."

Pillow laughed. "Oh, Vinnie, you do make me smile." And he pretended to trip and nearly fell off the platform, rolling onto the ground. The Cataquerians roared with laughter.

But standing before the now happy crowd, Vinnie suddenly felt something entirely new. He watched Loops, chatting happily with Musette and other Cattonas, and he ached. As he thought about how much Loops had hurt him by sticking up for Sunny instead of him, Vinnie wondered if this new feeling was, dare he say it, love?

DOGGEROES

Up at Bellows Edge, Hans strolled around. He was very big, masculine, extremely white, and mischievous. At sixteen months old, he was still considered to be a puppy, and a very irritating one at that!

His parents, Rita and Hans, had landed on the island some years ago. They had first been spotted by the young wife of a wealthy, and much older, American businessman in Hong Kong. She insisted on having the puppies, so her husband gave in and the pups were brought aboard the couple's yacht. But upon learning that to take the puppies home to the United States they would need vaccinations and lots of paperwork and forms filled out and filed, the couple decided they couldn't be bothered.

Sailing past the island, they'd decided it would be a perfect place for the puppies to grow up and live happily and freely. So, they moored as close as possible to the island, tossed the pups overboard, and watched to see that they swam to shore. Happily, they did. And the young wife shed a few tears, which left her husband thinking how sweet and considerate she was, and then returned to her sunbathing, forgetting about the puppies completely.

Rita and Ralph soon settled into their new territory, which rested snugly beneath Diggets Cave. They were welcomed by Growl, a young West Highland Terrier. Growl was firm, strong, and kind. He immediately took to both pups and formed a close bond with Ralph, who, as he grew, became an amazing hunter. Ralph could catch anything.

Ralph was also fair to the other dogs. He never retaliated or fought when disputes broke out; instead, he would reason with unruly dogs. And like Growl, he could instill respect for he was intelligent and fearless.

The dog's territory was filled with many different breeds. These breeds developed because dogs had bred with wild dogs already on the island. At Bellows Edge, fighting amongst the packs was not accepted. From its beginning, it was a place where unfairness and disrespectful behavior was not tolerated. Over time, Bellows Edge grew into a strong and respected territory in which good values were important.

Today, while Hans strolled around, looking for something to get into, Ralph stretched out his long legs and lifted his narrow head. Sniffing in all directions, he looked very regal. His black and white coat was as mixed as a rug and as neat and coarse as well. His eyes were very narrow and jet-black, like shiny buttons.

Earlier that day, Ralph, who had decided it was time to take Hans out hunting, had discussed his plans with Rita.

"Don't you think it's a bit too early for that?" she asked hesitantly. "Don't you think Hans is still a bit excitable and awkward to be going to Bellows Pond?"

"He's a hunter, Rita, a born hunter. Yes, he's young and still playful, but somewhere inside him is a great hunter. His instincts are just waiting to come through, and they will once he gets the scent, the rush, and the yearning to hunt. And he will, Rita. That's why he must go out with me."

Rita gazed at Ralph with her big, chocolate eyes. Her fur was a silky grey, soft and warm. It glistened day and night. "Have you talked to Growl about this?"

"I'm going to visit him now. I thought I'd take Hans with me."

Rita nodded. "I guess you know best, dear. I just worry, that's all. Have you spoken to Hans yet about your plans to take him on this big adventure?"

"No, not yet, but I am sure he will be fine. We need another hunter in the pack, and he knows that."

"What about me?" piped up Ditty, who had appeared out of nowhere. Ditty was like that. He and Hans had been born only weeks apart, but Ralph had found Ditty by the shore one early morning, covered in sand, and with twigs and broken seashells stuck in his fur. Ralph immediately knew that the hungry, frail pup had been abandoned. Ralph had raced back home, carrying Ditty in his mouth. And when Rita saw him, she immediately fell in love with Ditty. She could tell he was just a few weeks old, like Hans. His little eyes could barely open and he wiggled like a worm as she held him tight. Rita nursed him with Hans until they were both big enough to eat on their own. Rita often wondered what had happened to Ditty's mother. Rita hoped she was safe and wished she could know that Ditty was now with a family that truly loved him.

As Hans and Ditty grew up, they became inseparable, but couldn't have been more different. Where Hans was big and bumbling, Ditty was small and quick. He looked like a longhaired rabbit whose fur had gone curly. He had tiny, wispy ears and a short, stumpy tail. He was the color of caramel with dark grey streaks. And he was fast, agile, and full of energy.

Now, waiting for Ralph to tell him if he could become a hunter, too, Ditty bounced and bobbed with his usual energy.

Rita smiled at him. "Oh, Ditty, tots, we really need you here."

Ralph told Ditty, gently, "Listen to your, mum, Ditty. She knows best."

131

"Oh, I guess so," Ditty sighed.

"I'll get Hans and we'll head up to Diggets Cave," Ralph told Rita. She watched Ralph walk away, and when she turned to look at Ditty, he was gone. This didn't surprise Rita, for Ditty was always scampering off.

Ditty was, in fact, heading for Diggets Cave. He thought it'd be fun to be there when Hans and Ralph arrived. After all, Hans often told Ditty that perhaps he was a cousin to Growl, which always made Ditty rather excited. But Hans would also tell Ditty not to mention this to anyone since it could cause problems in the pack. He'd wink at Ditty and say, "Do you understand?" And Ditty would wag his stumpy little tail and reply, "Sure do, Hans."

Growl, the pack leader and Top Doggeroe, had lived at Diggets Cave, which sat high above the island, for many years. Living so high up had never been a problem for Growl, since craggy mountains posed no problem for a West Highland White Terrier. Stocky, short, and relatively small in size, Growl was fierce and could instill fear into any dog with just a look. He never had to fight for his position, and those in his pack respected him. Growl never bred or had a mate, for being his pack's leader and advisor took all his time and energy. He loved his pack mates deeply and with compassion, and they loved and respected him back. Growl taught his pack, and especially the pups, about the other animals on the island. He would tell them stories about Vinnie, and how Growl himself had a few near misses with Vinnie's knife-like claws. Growl warned the youngsters that Vinnie could hook a pup up in seconds and scrape an eye out before you could even blink.

But there had been talk lately that Growl, who was quite old, might soon be gone. When he called meetings to be updated on daily events, he would often wobble on his feet or doze off during them, causing an uncomfortable silence. But everyone respected and loved him so, they would simply wait patiently for him to wake up, and no one would ever leave his presence without his consent.

When Ditty reached Diggets Cave, he spotted Growl sitting outside the entrance to the cave, still as a statute. These days Growl rarely moved around much. His coat, once white as fresh snow, had begun to resemble days-old snow. Growl often felt like he was melting away, and though he often stumbled on his paws, he was too proud to talk of his aches and pains. Today he sat, thinking about how he must provide for his pack.

Ditty, meanwhile, watched Growl, thinking about how similar they were, how much they looked alike. *If only Growl knew, like Hans always said, that perhaps we are related*, thought Ditty, *perhaps then I could be of use around here. Oh, why doesn't' anyone take me seriously?*

Suddenly Ditty heard something and started yapping nonstop, which echoed throughout the caves and straight into Growl's old ears.

"Would you be quiet!" shouted Growl. "It's only Ralph and Hans. Can't you smell your own dogs before you hear them? Will you ever learn, you foolish pup?"

Ditty crawled forward toward Growl in a submissive position. "I am sorry, I forgot to sniff before I barked," he said. And then he leapt up and ran off to greet Hans, who was now bounding toward Ditty.

"Wooooooooooo!" said Hans as he knocked into Ditty, sending him flying into the air.

"Whaaaa, hey!" Ditty yelped as he went sliding across the dry ground, sending up a great cloud of orange dust, which floated around Growl like a spray of perfume.

"Oh, you silly pups," Ralph muttered, with a shake of his head. "Perhaps Rita was right after all, and Hans isn't mature enough to be taught to hunt."

Ralph moved to Growl, and they touched paws. Growl was always pleased to see Ralph, for they went back a long way and had great respect for one another. Ralph, a born hunter, and Growl, a born leader, had long worked as a team. They had seen many changes and faced many troubles on the island over the years, and still held command amongst the pack.

"So, what brings you here to see this old boy, then?" Growl asked Ralph, smiling.

"It's Hans. I think it's time I took him down to Bellows Pond. We need another hunter and he needs training. A dog that big could be trouble if he doesn't learn to obey and to be tolerant of others. The excitement and satisfaction of the kill will keep him focused and free from causing trouble. He won't need to seek pleasure within his territory if he learns to keep killing for survival rather than fun."

"I agree." Growl nodded. "Hans needs focus and direction. He is coming into his time of resistance and challenges when he will want to fight back to win an argument. Hunting is the only way to break him of this. Without rules to guide him, he could be trouble. He is one of the biggest dogs I've ever seen so he will make a great hunter, as you are, Ralph. If anyone can keep him, it's you. We really don't want to lose him. He's a fine animal. He just needs training."

Growl looked up to see a cloud of dust billowing before them. Ditty was pegged down onto Hans's neck. Hans was lying on his back, sprawled out, paws on either side of him while Ditty's little back legs raced in mid-air like a rabbit running for its life. Hans was walloping the ground with his paws, moving from side to side, and pretending he couldn't get up because Ditty was far too strong.

"Oh, you got me this time, Ditty," Hans said, and grinned.

Growl chuckled. "Hans has good in him like you, Ralph. He will be fine."

Ralph nodded. "Then we will set off tomorrow morning early."

29

RESTLESS CAMP TALK

There was a lot of tension in the colony, mostly because Vinnie was again being his typical angry, aggressive, and thoroughly unpleasant self.

Tibby and Pillow, who were sitting in the sun, were both thinking about this. Tibby was fed up dealing with the playground politics, while Pillow felt frustrated at the hierarchy in the colony. He was uncomfortable with the notion that a group of simple-minded Cattons could dictate how others lived in their own community. *We need to promote more democracy, but how?* Pillow wondered. *How can I get the rest of these Cattons to wake up, stand up for themselves, and live their lives independent of Vinnie? I will request another vote, a vote for freedom of speech, a vote for individual choice and individual rights. I will turn this community around if it's the last thing I do! But before we do this, we need to get Vernon Mickey, Danny, and Spit free of Vinnie's spell.*

Feeling he might be able to think better outside of the noise and bustle colony, Pillow turned to Tibby. "Hey, old boy, fancy a stroll? I was thinking of heading up to one of the highest points on the island.

"How far do you think that will be?" Tibby looked up at the rocky shapes.

"A few miles, perhaps. I bet the view is amazing from up there, though. What do you say?"

"Why not?" Tibby replied. "It'll break up the boredom of the day. And what about Musette, shall we ask her to come, too?"

"Oh, let's not bother her," Pillow said. "She so loves spending time with the kittens and mums." He suddenly looked sad. "She would have made a great mum."

Tibby nodded. "I suppose living with people taught us that it's not necessary to breed. But living here in the wild, it's vital to survival."

"Oh well, what's done is done." Pillow sighed.

"Let's go, dear fellow." Tibby touched Pillow's shoulder reassuringly.

They headed out of the colony and were soon skipping through lush green plants. The air around them began to feel a lot cooler.

"Ahh, this is refreshing," said Pillow.

"I do believe I am actually losing weight," Tibby announced with pride. "I am getting so fit from all of the exercise and healthy food we have been blessed with on the island."

They had been walking for over an hour when they began the climb to the top of the island.

As they jumped upward, they noticed fresh, clear water trickling down, in between the rock face, towards them.

"Oh, look at Mother Nature's most precious gift, water," Pillow said. He put his paw into the stream of water. He loved the feel of the pure liquid, which seemed to cool and soothe his troubled mind. He became playful, trying to snatch up droplets of water as if they were invisible flies.

"You'll never catch it." Tibby laughed.

"Yes, I will!" said Pillow, leaping and splashing.

The sound of the water was familiar and comforting, for it reminded them of the back gardens in England, with their fountains and ponds.

"I do love being away from the colony. I think we should stay here a while. I just want to listen to the water," Tibby said.

"And I just want to play with the it," Pillow replied, still mesmerized by the crystal-clear droplets splashing onto his paws.

Tibby lay down in a mass of soft green vines, which had grown in a perfectly round circle. "This is bliss. We must do this more often." And he yawned and was very quickly in a deep sleep.

Pillow continued chasing the flow of water as if he were after an invisible mouse. He ran blissfully along the stream, unaware of anyone or anything around him.

Hans and Ralph were sitting still after their busy day of hunting. A medium-sized boar lay next to them. On his first day out hunting, Hans had secured his first kill. He was grinning, feeling terribly proud that he had proven he could provide for the pack.

"Come on, Hans," said Ralph, "best we head back home. You take this fine fellow you killed."

Hans proudly picked the boar up in his mouth and threw it over his back and the two set off, chatting about how Growl, despite his small size, had killed many boars and somehow carried them back to Diggets Cave on his own.

"I don't know how long Growl has left, Hans," Ralph said, looking thoughtful. "He is looking so weak and weary these days."

"He still scares me," Hans said with total respect. "And I bet he'll keep going for a long time yet."

Wishful thinking, Ralph thought. "You never know. Growl could outlive us all."

Pillow's eyes hadn't left the water's flow. In fact, he had spotted a tadpole, which was heading fast and furiously away from his paws, along a small stream winding its way through some rocks. This had allowed the fast-flowing water to escape, and to loop its way along the ground all the way to its final destination, a cool pond full of frogs and toads.

Pillow pounced in and out of the stream as he tried to catch the tadpole. He was becoming as wet as a fish himself, and from afar, it looked like he was playing hopscotch. Finally, he secured the little tadpole beneath his paw. He could feel it wiggling and wobbling as it tried to escape.

"Oh, go on then, off you go," Pillow said, and he raised his paw, setting the tadpole free. But when Pillow raised his head, he found himself facing two very big dogs that had a very dead animal with them.

Pillow felt a lump in his throat and his life began to flash before him. He thought of Musette. He couldn't take his eyes off of the dead boar, thinking, *That will be me next.*

He took a breath and looked at the dogs. "Hello," he said, trying to hide his fear. "I haven't seen you fellows before."

He remembered Vinnie's stories about the wild Doggeroes that ate cats after they had skinned them alive. Pillow decided to remain absolutely still since running might stir the dogs into a frenzy. If he stayed calm, he thought he might be able to negotiate an escape.

"Hi!" Hans said. He'd never spoken to a Catton before.

"Hello," Ralph added, for he wasn't sure what to say either.

"I am Pillow. I am not local. I fell off of a cargo ship with my Cattona and my friend, who's just upstream resting. And here I am here now with you in the rain forest having a stroll like I don't have a care in the world." Pillow spoke so fast he could hardly catch breath. His paws were shaking, and his claws gripped the dirt beneath him. His tail was moving like a long worm, and Hans couldn't take his eyes off it.

"Relax," Ralph told Pillow. "We have no interest in harming you or your friend. As you can see, we have our food and we never harm or hurt just for fun.

Hans's tail was wagging furiously. He walked slowly up to Pillow and began to sniff him all over. Then he licked Pillow straight across the face, smothering him with curiosity and kindness.

"Now, now," Ralph told Hans, "I'm sure he has had a wash. Leave him be, young man."

But Hans just couldn't. He was still a pup and he wanted to know how Pillow smelt and wanted to sense his energy as well.

"Steady on," Pillow said with a smile, and he grabbed Hans's ear with his paw, suddenly feeling like a kitten wanting to play with a big toy. But then Pillow composed himself and coughed to clear his throat. "So, I guess you are one of the dangerous Doggeroes," he told Hans, feeling a bit less nervous but still mindful that these two dogs were very powerful.

Hans, who just couldn't stop sniffing Pillow, excitedly cried, "I am!" and pushed Pillow down to the ground. With a gentle paw, Hans prodded Pillow like he was made of candyfloss. Pillow wrapped his paws around Hans and began gently kicking into Hans's big neck with his back paws.

"That's enough, Hans," said Ralph sternly, much to Pillow's relief. Hans let him go. Pillow rolled over and sat up. He began dusting himself off, while trying to look a little more serious.

A few yards away, Tibby woke up, stretching and yawning, quite refreshed from his peaceful snooze. Then he realized he could hear Pillow talking to someone and thought perhaps some of Vinnie's friends had followed them. He moved toward the sound of the voices. Then he saw Hans standing very close to Pillow, and Ralph nearby.

"Oh my days!" Tibby began to hiss, and his body went rigid. He wasn't sure if he should try to save Pillow himself or run for help.

It's okay, Tibby!" shouted Pillow. "We are just chatting, honestly. Tibby, do come and meet Hans and Ralph."

And before long, the two cats and the two dogs were chatting away, exchanging stories and learning about each other. It was a wonderful day, and Pillow felt stronger than ever before.

BONES TO STIR SOUP

Vinnie had always done very well in convincing the Cataquerians that the dogs were evil and dangerous. He had made up wicked stories about having seen kittens on sticks being roasted over hot fires. No cats ever dared to venture anywhere near Diggets Cave, for they believed they would surely never return.

The Doggeroes had always stayed far away from Willows Rock. They did not need to kill Cataquerians for there was plenty of prey on the island. Plus, they didn't need any one-eyed dogs roaming around.

Pillow and Tibby arrived back at Willows Rock feeling happier than before. They now knew life didn't have to be lived within the realm of the colony; the island was bigger than that. Now they just had to convince the other Cataquerians.

Musette was sitting in the hut when Pillow returned, preening herself and purring happily. Pillow started to tell her all about his and Tibby's adventure that day and what they had discovered.

"If only I could convince everyone that the dogs on this Island are no threat to the Cataquerians, things would be so very different around here," he told Musette. "We could all roam freely, hunt further, and not live in fear of the Doggeroes."

"I don't know, darling," Musette said. "What if Vinnie tries to prove you wrong? You know how cunning and manipulative he is."

Tibby, who'd heard the mention of Vinnie's name, appeared to ask, "What's he done now?"

"It's what he hasn't done, Tibby," Pillow said. "Vinnie hasn't told the colony the truth about the Doggeroes."

"You mustn't spend so much time on Vinnie, he's not worth the energy," Tibby said. "Just be kinder and more understanding towards him."

"Are you going as soft as the sand, Tibby?" Pillow asked.

"No, I am just saying he is a victim of circumstances. Heaven knows what sort of upbringing he had."

"Well, that's no excuse for him being so wicked all the time," Musette said. "And knowing his history won't change him."

"That's a bit harsh, Musette," Pillow said. "Everyone can change. Even Vinnie."

"For heaven's sake, make your mind up, Pillow. One minute you can't stand him and the next you're defending him! I give up, I really do," Musette said, shaking her head.

One day the air seemed to change on the island. It became silent and creepily still. And the skies turned dark grey, a color no one had ever before seen.

Tibby, sitting outside his cave, suddenly remembered sitting with Mrs. Maple one day, watching a story about hurricanes on the television. *I wonder if a hurricane is going to hit the island*, he thought, and called Pillow over for a chat.

"Listen, old chap, have you noticed how still the island has become? I can't even hear the sound of birds singing, and I feel quite restless, like I want to run away."

"I did notice how the air has changed and the sky's growing darker," Pillow said. "Perhaps we should discuss this with

Vinnie and the others." And so they he and Pillow headed to Willows Circle to find Vinnie, who was there most days.

On the way, Pillow and Tibby came upon Mickey, Spit, and Danny.

"Hey, what's new? You coming for a coco juice with us? We're meeting Vinnie and Vernon," Mickey said.

"How cozy," said Tibby with sarcasm. "Can't wait. A boys' night out."

"Boys' night out for us," chuckled Spit. "but isn't it your bedtime, old cat?"

Tibby just ignored Spit. He was more concerned with the breezeless, warm moist air. He felt it now harder to breathe.

Mickey noticed Tibby looking pale. "You okay?" he asked. "Spit was just joking. You really ain't that old."

Tibby looked to Pillow, who now said, "We should all go and sit down and have a chat. We really need to talk with you."

All three cats looked a bit puzzled but nodded.

They reached Willows Circle where they spotted Vernon sitting with Vinnie. Everyone sat down together.

"What is it now, Monkey Boy?" Vinnie asked. "Don't tell me you want us to start having cooking lessons?" He burst out laughing.

Pillow said, "No, Vinnie, but something terrible is going to happen on the island."

Vinnie screamed so loud that all the Cataquerians came running out of their huts from all directions.

"What on earth is going on?" Twinkles asked, reaching Tibby's side. She held a half-finished basket she was making from dried grass reeds.

Tibby smiled at her and Twinkles grinned back.

"OH MY!" Vinnie yelled. "The only terrible thing happening on this island is these two old cats flirting! *YUK!*"

And he shuddered.

By now Loops was standing next to Musette as Pillow addressed everyone. "Listen everyone, a hurricane is on its way. It will hit this island pretty soon and we need to take shelter."

"Oh, rotten suffering rats!" shouted Vinnie. "Who do you think you are, coming down here and telling us there's a bit of rain on its way. Do we look stupid?"

"A bit of rain is not what's coming. And the Cataquerians are at risk," said Pillow, not moving his eyes from Vinnie.

"There you go again," Vinnie said, "you and your crazy nonsense. I know you're just trying to be the leader when you're not! Stop interfering, Pillow, or I swear I will stop being so nice!"

"But Vinnie, aren't you feeling like you want to run? Can't you see how restless we all are? This is instinct, the instinct of our ancestors, of our breed, and we shouldn't ignore it." Pillow tried to reason with Vinnie. "Believe me I know what not listening to your gut can do. When I left our safe cabin aboard that cargo ship, my gut told me, *No, don't do it, don't leave this cabin*. But I did anyway and look where I am now."

"Oh, shut up! You're insane, you're mad crazy!" Vinnie's claws twitched with anger.

But Pillow continued. "We need to go up to Diggets Cave. It's the safest place on the island."

Danny now spoke up. "Listen, Vinnie, obviously a storm is coming, you can see from the sky."

"And obviously Pillow loves to make things up. And now he wants us to go up to Diggets Cave until it stops raining?! Go up there with those mangy, vicious, crazy Doggeroes?!"

But no one answered Vinnie. Instead, they just continue to stare at him.

"I mean how many storms have we had here?" Vinnie asked, feeling increasingly frustrated. "Hundreds, if not more every year. They come and go, so what is the big deal?"

"Tibby, tell them all about the silence, the fact that the birds have stopped singing, and all the things that are happening now. Have they ever happened before on the island?" Pillow said.

"Not like this, not like this at all!" Danny said. Vinnie glared at him, but Danny ignored him. "What harm can it do just to listen?" Danny was thinking about his family; he just wanted them all to be safe.

"Harm!" Vinnie screamed. "Harm! We will be in the guts of a pack of idiot dogs tonight, crunched like fish bones and swallowed alive, that's what harm it'll be!"

"I am confident a hurricane is on its way," Tibby announced. "I learned all about them whilst I was watching television with my dear companion, Mrs. Maple. We really need to warn the others. These types of tropical storms are very rare and dangerous. We must find shelter and time is running out. We need a plan and we need it now."

"I will go and talk to Ralph to see if we can take shelter in Diggets Cave. Musette, stay here and spread the word to the others," Pillow announced.

"Are you insane?!" Vinnie screamed, spitting, hissing, and jumping around like he was standing on hot coals.

Oh dear, thought Pillow. "Please calm down, Vinnie. You're going to do yourself an injury. Calm down," he said, until Vinnie finally did, but he still glared at Pillow.

"Don't you know what that pack of savages will do to us if we go anywhere near them? They will chew us up and use our bones to stir soup!" Vinnie exclaimed.

"Talk about dramatic," Musette muttered. "You do need to

get a grip, Vinnie."

"Look, Vinnie, we have met Ralph and Hans, two of the biggest dogs living up at Diggets Cave," Pillow said. "And to be fair, they seemed decent enough chaps. We sat and talked to them for a while about our lives and about theirs. I think this would be a great opportunity for all of us to meet."

"Listen to me, you dizzy fools," Vinnie hissed. "It's a trap! Those empty rock heads will rip us all to shreds if we so much as breathe their air."

By now all the Cataquerians had gathered around. They respected Pillow and Tibby, but none of them had ever been up to Diggets Cave.

"Well," said Pillow firmly, "Tibby and I are going up there now. We have no time to lose arguing over soup bones. Musette, I want you to do your best to talk some sense into the girls. They should listen to you. We'll be back as soon as we can."

"Go ahead, you fools!" Vinnie laughed. "It was nice knowing you before you were turned into Doggeroe food!"

"I didn't know you cared," Pillow told Vinnie with a smile. "Come on, Tibby. Let's go." And off they went.

Vinnie turned to Musette with a grin. "So, sweet cheeks, looks like you're gonna be a Cattloner. But don't worry, it won't be for long."

"A Cattloner indeed. I'd rather be a Cattloner than a *cata*strophe," Musette replied.

"I bet," Vinnie said, looking a bit puzzled. But then he thought, *She sure likes me*, completely missing the fact that Musette rolled her eyes.

GROWL MEETS PILLOW

Growl was sitting outside his cave, looking out across the hills to the still, calm ocean beyond. He felt restless and full of energy, but he couldn't run. He was at the highest point on the island and he knew his place was here. If he had wings, he would fly, for he felt so much power surging through his body. He sensed this was going to be a bad storm, but he knew the pack would be safe in their territory.

Nearly all the dogs were up in the cave. They sensed something wasn't right and knew a storm was approaching. Things were noisy and lively. Growl insisted that Ralph calm things down since pups were running about wildly, playing, tussling, and chasing each other, and some were even trying to scamper off.

Suddenly things got even louder as an orchestra of yapping began. It was almost deafening.

Growl slowly and calmly stepped out of the cave, worried there might be a family of cobras lurking there, ready to pounce. But to Growl's amazement, he saw two Cataquerians waving large palm leaves and hissing like snakes to ward of the puppies who were jumping all around and up at them like fleas.

"We come in peace!" shouted Pillow. "Please! We need to speak with Ralph."

Growl barked so loudly and sternly that all the pups headed back to their own caves. "Come forward! No harm will come to you," Growl said.

"Hello. You must be Growl," said Pillow.

"Yes, I am. What brings you up here?"

"This is Tibby, my friend," Pillow informed. "We are–" but he was suddenly interrupted as Ralph came running forward.

"Pillow, what's up? Is everything all right? Has that Vinnie threatened to kill you yet?" Ralph asked.

"You clearly have met before," Growl said, surprised he hadn't been told about this.

Ralph looked embarrassed. "Yes, we have. I will explain later."

Growl turned back to Pillow. "What do you want?"

"Tibby will explain, for he knows more than I," Pillow said.

"I believe a hurricane is on its way here, one like you have never experienced before," Tibby began. "That is why it's so still and hardly a sound can be heard except the ocean."

Growl nodded. "Hmmm. Yes, I thought as much. I can feel it in my bones."

"Would it be possible to borrow one of your caves until the storm passes?" Pillow now asked. "We have very young kittens and without shelter, they are bound to get swept away."

"And Vinnie?" Growl asked coldly. "He is not welcome here. He has done nothing but try to cause trouble."

Pillow nodded but remained quiet.

There was a long pause. Finally Growl spoke. "All I ask is that you come quietly, keep to yourselves, and leave as soon as the storm is over."

"We will do so. Thank you, thank you, indeed," said Pillow gratefully. "And what about your pack?" He had noticed some very mean-looking dogs sitting silently nearby.

"You made it this far," said Ralph. "Vinnie's the only Cataquerian who wouldn't make it up here alive."

"Vinnie's really all mouth and no fur," Tibby now said.

Growl laughed and then nodded. "You have our word," and he stepped over to Tibby and Pillow and crossed paws with them.

"You're a true gentleman, sir," Pillow said. "Thank you."

Growl decided to call a meeting for he could hear snarling among the pack. When all the dogs had gathered, he spoke. "It has become evident, given our feelings of restlessness today, that a great storm is approaching, which is of grave danger to us all. I have given one of our caves to the Cataquerians so that they may take shelter. I don't want to hear a word about this. But everyone must stay in your own caves until the hurricane passes. I have a feeling it will change this island."

Ditty started running around. "Does that mean we can play with the kittens? Oh boy, I can't wait! I won't be the smallest! I'll finally be the biggest!" he cried with excitement.

Rita laughed. "No, Ditty. We must leave them be. They will be far too scared of us."

"And so they should be," added Hans. "We could eat them all for snacks."

"Well, maybe not Tibby," Ralph added, laughing. "He would be a bit tough to chew on given his age."

But Growl was not amused. "This is not a time for jokes, everyone. We must prepare for this storm." And with that, Growl moved slowly off towards his cave.

TAKING SHELTER

Musette addressed the other Cattonas who were looking worried and unsure. "We must take all the children up to Diggets Cave. We can trust Pillow. He would never put any of us in harm's way."

"I'm not sure about this," said Suzy Wing. "If the Doggeroes are not a threat to us, then why have so many kittens gone missing?"

"Because that's what kittens do when you turn your back for a second," said Musette, slightly frustrated for she knew they didn't have much time. The wind was picking up and her own instincts were urging her to flee.

Suddenly Pillow appeared, much to Musette 's relief.

"It's okay," Pillow told the Cattonas. "Growl has agreed to let us take shelter in Diggets Cave until the hurricane passes."

"OH MY WORD!" screamed Vinnie, who had been lying under the cloud-filled sky, trying to appear cool as a cucumber. *"UNBELIEVABLE!* They're going to lead us all to our deaths!"

"Oh be quiet, you silly coconut!" snapped Musette. "When have any one of you ever been attacked by a Doggeroe? Tell me that!" she insisted.

Loops, who was standing and listening quietly, felt empowered by Musette's willingness to stand up to Vinnie.

"Answer me!" Musette said again.

"Oh, here we go," Vinnie said. "The little firecracker's getting you all at it."

Musette's tail was swaying like a runaway ribbon in the wind. "I'm going up to Diggets Cave and that's that." She turned to Loops. "I urge you, Loops, to bring the others. If you stay, you will surely be swept away, lifted into the air, and thrown out to sea. Please, Loops!" Musette held Loops's shoulders firmly and stared into her eyes. "Do you trust me?" she asked, waiting for Loops to answer.

Loops stood still; her tiny frame held firmly by the friend she loved dearly. "Of course I trust you, Musette."

"Then what are you waiting for?" Musette asked with a wink.

"Let's go, everyone!" Loops shouted. "Come on, ladies. Take the children, bring food, and tell your Cattons to help as much as they can."

Vinnie looked Loops straight in the eye. "If you do this, Loops," he said slowly, "if you disobey me, I will no longer be your Catton and you will no longer have privileges of this colony. I mean it. I will cast you out. You will lose everything, your home and all your rights."

"This is not the time to think of yourself. This isn't about you, Vinnie. It's about the safety of us all, the kittens, and the entire colony. So, stop the bravado and help us."

Vinnie was speechless with fury. He stuttered, he spat, he paced, and he clawed at the ground like he was digging a tunnel. "Do you what you like, *ALL OF YOU!*" he raged, "Make the biggest mistake of your lives! I don't care about any of you! *YOU ARE WITHERING FOOLS.* I'll be fine here, you wait and see! I'll be right here when you get back!" Although Vinnie didn't say it, he intended to go to his secret underground hideaway where he keep his fermented coconut, dried meat, and tobacco leaves to wait out the storm.

But no one was listening for the wind had picked up and

the sky had darkened further. The women hurried away, leaving Vinnie behind.

Time was running out.

THE CATAQUERIANS MEET THE DOGGEROES

"**Okay,** everyone, make your way up to Diggets Cave as fast as you can," Pillow ordered. "Don't worry. They are expecting us, and they will all be in their own homes by now, keeping safe. They, too, know what's on the way. So let's go!"

By now the rain was pouring down and trees were swaying as the wind swirled around them. The sky was so dark it looked like it was dying from a force that had overtaken its heart.

As the cats headed up towards Diggets Cave. the mums grasping their little kittens in their mouths while the other female cats took one each, holding on to them gently but firmly. The wind had picked up speed and the trees were swaying and rustling, as if telling the Cattonas to hurry along with their precious cargo. The air was so warm it made them drowsy, and the growing rain pushed down on them with its looming power.

As they reached the top of the mountain, they struggled to climb onto the last rock, using every last bit of their strength.

"You can do it!" shouted Musette, as the Cattonas helped each other. All that mattered was getting the kittens to safety in the cave and out of harm's way.

When all the Cattonas and kittens reached Diggets Cave, they felt exhilarated and knew they had really accomplished something. Suddenly they all felt they could do anything from now on.

Inside the cave, the cats found fresh meat and clean bedding thanks to Rita and some of her friends who had gathered the supplies and set up the cave for their guests. Upon finding the cave made so homey and ready for them, the Cataquerians felt humbled and even a bit ashamed that they had ever harbored bad thoughts about the Doggeroes.

Musette, whose fur was soaked through, could have stayed out of the rain and harsh conditions. But instead she and Loops ushered everyone into the cave. Neither of them stopped running until everyone was safe.

Danny, Spit, and Vernon were directing other Cattons to exit their homes and head for the cave, while Pillow ushered more families to safety. Throughout the entire evacuation of the colony and the move to Diggets Cave, Tibby had been doing a head count. Finally, he was confident everyone was accounted for and safe, with the exception of Vinnie.

From the shelter of the cave, everyone – except the kittens, who were tired, hungry, and only wanted to feed – could see branches, leaves, and flying debris soar past the cave's entrance as the hurricane picked up speed.

Pillow sighed, glad to have Musette safely by his side. Then he addressed everyone. "We will leave first thing in the morning."

"But why?" Socks asked. "I want to see the puppies!"

"Because I promised Growl we would leave right after the storm, and that is that, young man," Pillow told Socks.

Socks was black except for his white socks, which started at his feet and reached his little knees. He was one of Susie Wing's children and was very mischievous. He loved to climb trees and sometimes would go so high he would become stuck. He would then cry until a passing Cataquerian would rescue him.

Socks sulked. "But I'm bored. I want to play."

"Not now, Socks," said his mother. "There is plenty to do." And she took a vine out of her basket in which she had placed some food and began to drag it around the ground. Immediately all the kittens came running and tried to latch onto the vine, tumbling over each other until one kitten finally grabbed the vine with its little claw.

Tibby groaned. *Oh dear, I don't know how I am going to cope with this all night.*

The male cats sat together chatting, although Pillow was doing most of the talking. He had gained even more of the other Cattons' respect. And he was beginning to feel a real sense of purpose on the island. Deep within, he believed that Musette's falling overboard had been no accident.

"I wonder how many Doggeroes are living here," Danny wondered out loud.

"I believe between eighteen to twenty," Tibby informed.

"Not that many really," Vernon added. "One for each of us."

"Oh, come on, said Pillow, "you don't actually believe all of that nonsense about kittens being eaten alive, do you?"

"Hello, everyone."

All the cats turned toward the cave's opening where Rita and Ralph had appeared. "Are you all okay in here?" Rita asked.

"Oh yes, thank you. And it was so kind of you to leave us food and bedding," Musette said.

"You're very welcome," said Rita. "It's not easy having young ones, and so many of them as well," she said, smiling as she looked at the kittens hissing, spitting, and waving their tails.

"Oh take no notice, they're just being youngsters," said Pillow.

Ralph laughed. "As long as you're all fine."

Danny, Vernon, and Spit were silent. They didn't really

know what to think anymore. They could see with their own eyes that these dogs meant them no harm.

"Good night, then," Ralph said. "Sleep well." And with that, he and Rita left.

The cats all began to feel tired. It had been a long day. They finally felt relaxed enough to sleep and they all went off into their own spaces, some cuddling with kittens, and others on their own.

NIGHTTIME RESCUE

Everyone was snug, warm, and asleep in both caves, except for the few kittens and puppies still busy playing. They were mischievously creeping about, stepping over long legs and tails neatly curled under or sprawled out as straight as bamboo.

In the cats' cave, Socks and Scratch, a pale, ginger-colored kitten with blue eyes and white stripes, were whispering about the Doggeroes.

"Oh, I'm not scared of them," said Scratch.

"Oh yes you are," Socks teased. "I bet you're as scared as a mouse."

"I am not!" Scratch began to paw and prod Socks until they were rolling about like tumbleweed in the wind.

"Shhhhh," Susie Wing said, yawning as she woke. "You two will wake up the others. Go to sleep for goodness sake."

"Okay, Mum, sorry, Mum," said Socks as he pretended to bed down for the night. But when he saw his mum turn away from him, he whispered to Scratch. "Let's go outside and see if we can see any Doggeroes."

"Oh, I don't know about that," Scratch replied.

"Are you chicken?"

"No, of course not," Scratch told Socks. "I just don't want to get blown away."

"We won't," Socks promised. "Just hold onto me."

So they popped their heads outside of the cave. The wind was howling, but it wasn't raining heavily, only misting.

"It's not so bad out here," Socks said. "Why was everyone making such a fuss about this storm?"

Scratch shrugged and followed Socks as he stepped out of the cave.

As they ventured outside, they felt a gust of wind.

"Did you feel that?" Scratch asked.

"It's nothing, come on. Let's go," Socks said, and he and Scratch began to make their way to the next cave where the Doggeroes were. The wind tried to force them back, but they kept going, pushing their way forward until they reached the cave.

Once inside, Socks and Scratch saw big dogs lying flat out. Some were snoring while others were asleep, but their legs were moving as if they were running for their lives.

Ditty was sitting by his mum, Rita, who was fast asleep. When he spotted Socks and Scratch, he started to wag his tail and then raced over to them.

"Hello," Ditty said, "what are you two doing, being up and about in this storm?"

"We decided to go exploring. Do you want to come?" Socks asked.

"Oh, yes please," Ditty said.

"Come on then!" Scratch encouraged, and Ditty moved with Scratch and Socks toward the opening to the cave. They all peered outside. The rain was now heavier, and water was cascading wildly down the rocks.

"Wow, look at all the water," Socks said.

"Wow, that's amazing!" Ditty shouted. "I bet I could cross over to the other side! Come on, it will be fun!"

All three ran out of the dogs' cave and toward the rock ledge. The rain was pouring heavily now, and the water running down the face of the cliff had turned into a waterfall.

Ditty, Scratch, and Socks could barely hear each other given the roaring sounds of water and rain.

"Oh, I don't like being this wet," Scratch said, for he was now feeling very nervous. The wind was raging against his body and he was slipping and falling into deep mud. "I think we should go back," he said as he swallowed more of the water beating into his little face.

Socks ignored Scratch for he wanted to see Ditty cross the rocks and then follow him. "Go inside then, Scratch, if you're scared of a bit of wind," Socks shouted.

Scratch tried to turn back but he couldn't fight the wind, which had turned wilder. He felt so frightened. He was being pushed toward the waterfall. He grabbed at the wet vines hanging from the tall swaying trees, but they were flapping, flying, and twisting him around. *"I CAN'T KEEP HOLDING ON!"* he screamed.

Socks, too, was being swept up in the wind, which had suddenly started to spiral. Ditty leapt up and grabbed his tail as he started to get sucked up into the air. Ditty pulled Socks to the ground, sat on top of him, and began to howl as loud as he possibly could.

Inside the dogs' cave, Rita woke up suddenly. "What's that?" she said, straining to hear. Then her heart started to beat rapidly. "Ditty? Ditty!" She moved over to Ralph and pushed at him with her paw. "Ralph, wake up! Ditty's gone and I can hear him howling!"

Ralph jumped to his feet. Hans was now by his side. Noticing the other dogs waking up, Ralph said, "Stay here, everyone. Hans and I will go. Come on, Hans, we have no time to waste."

In the cave next door, Musette had also woken up. "Pillow, do you hear howling? One of the dogs must be in trouble."

160

Pillow quickly got up and hurried outside.

There, he met Ralph and Hans as they exited their cave, and all of them moved toward the ledge. The violent rain was pounding their bodies, and, cat and dog alike, they all had to use all their strength to move toward the ledge.

Ditty was losing his balance. He knew he couldn't keep still much longer, for the force of the wind and rain was pushing him toward the edge of the ledge, into the waterfall and the raging waters below.

Ralph spotted Ditty first. *"HOLD ON, SON!"* he yelled.

At that moment, Pillow saw Scratch fly past the tops of the rapids. Ditty saw this, too, and couldn't believe his eyes. *Oh no!* he thought, knowing that if he moved, Socks would surely be swept away as well.

Ralph leapt up and caught Scratch in his mouth just as Ditty suddenly slipped, exposing Socks, and fell into the torrent of water. Without missing a beat, Ralph tossed Scratch into the air, in the direction of his cave. Scratch landed right outside it, got up, and rushed inside to safety.

Ralph, Pillow, and Hans rushed over to the ledge. Hans reached it first and put a big paw atop of Socks to steady him. Then, just as his father had done with Scratch, Hans picked Socks up in his mouth and flipped him into the air, in the direction of the cats' cave. Just as Scratch had done, Socks got up and, crying, ran inside as fast as he could.

Pillow screamed down to Ditty, *"HOLD ON!"* and then turned to Ralph. "I'm going into the water! Hold onto me!"

As Pillow flung himself downward, Ralph grabbed his tail and held Pillow just above the raging waters.

Pillow couldn't see a thing, but he plunged his paws into the water, searching for Ditty Finding nothing, Pillow screamed up to Ralph, *"GET ME DOWN FURTHER!"*

So, Ralph lowered Pillow closer into the torrent.

Through the wall of water, Pillow spotted Ditty who was tumbling like a rag dog in the raging water. Pillow managed to grab Ditty's tail. "Pull us up!" Pillow screamed to Ralph.

Ralph pulled with all his might as Pillow held firmly onto Ditty, who was whimpering and shaking. With a greave heave, Ralph hauled Pillow and Ditty up to the ledge. Pillow, bent over, paws on his knees, breathed in an out heavily, trying to catch his breath, as Ditty shook and cried.

"Are the kittens okay?" Ditty spluttered.

"Yes," said Pillow, gently tapping Ditty on the shoulder. "They're just fine, a bit wet but fine."

Ralph lifted up Ditty, who was looking very timid and sorry for himself, by the scruff of his neck, and carried him back to the entrance to the dogs' cave. Pillow and Hans followed.

"Go inside," Ralph told Ditty sternly. "I will deal with you later." And then he turned to Pillow. "Thank you for saving my son. I shall always be in your debt."

"And thank you for saving those kittens. I'm sorry they started it all."

Ralph sighed. "Well, I suppose kids will be kids," he said and turned to Hans. He just shrugged, as both Pillow and Ralph shook their heads and chuckled.

"Well, this has been more than a storm, said Tibby who was waiting anxiously for Pillow by the entrance of the cave. "It has been a revelation."

NEW BEGINNINGS

Ralph woke up with Rita asleep next to him. The only sounds he could hear were the gentle snoring of his fellow pack mates, and the deep breaths and little yelps as some paws were running in their dreams.

Ralph shook his head as if to clear it. Then he thought of last night's events. He couldn't believe Ditty had been so careless and stupid. It was time to have a talk with him. Ralph looked around. "Ditty?" he called out sternly. But scanning the entire cave, Ralph realized there wasn't a puppy in sight. Only adults were stirring and stretching. He turned to Rita. "Wake up," he said, gently pawing her.

"What it is, darling?" She yawned.

"There are no puppies," Ralph said.

Rita immediately jumped up, concerned, but then she heard lots of happy yelping and yapping. "I think they're all outside playing, Ralph."

Together they walked outside. The sun was shining, the sky was blue, and all signs of the storm had vanished. And there, before Ralph and Rita, was an army of kittens and puppies running about, playing and laughing together, with such harmony and joy that Rita's and Ralph's hearts could not help but sing in tune with this beautiful sight.

"Oh my," Rita said, "things will never be the same again around here."

"No, they never will be," mused Ralph.

"I am surprised Growl is not up to see this," Rita noted.

Probably just as well, Ralph thought. *Growl might think those old eyes of his were playing tricks on him.*

Pillow, Musette, Tibby, Danny, and Spit all suddenly appeared, wondering where the kittens had all gone but relieved that the storm had passed.

"Just look at them," Musette said, clutching her paws to her chest with an overwhelming feeling of love for both kittens and puppies.

"I know," Rita said, "I think we may have double trouble! But I do hope to see you all again soon."

"Now, now, ladies," said Ralph. "One drama is enough to last us a while."

"Indeed," Tibby said, "but it's been a great pleasure and one we will never forget."

Hans came rushing over from the cave, his usual bouncy self. He began to lick Pillow happily, but Pillow laughed and pushed Hans gently away.

"I had a good wash last night, thank you very much," he said laughing.

"Indeed," Ralph said. "I thought you had grown a pair of flippers."

Pillow crossed paws with Ralph and Hans, telling them, "I can't thank you enough. You surely saved many lives, if not all of ours, by allowing us to stay in the cave last night."

"And again, I am in debt to you, Pillow, for saving our son. Let's hope we cross paths again," Ralph said, as Rita smiled at Pillow.

Hans was now chatting with Tibby. "I guess we can go exploring further now," he said excitedly. "I love the kittens! They're so much fun to be around. And I want to meet Vinnie, I really do."

"I don't know about that, young man," replied Tibby. "Vinnie's nothing more than a thug who likes to bully everyone."

"Oh, I could handle Vinnie," Hans said.

"Not without a fight," Ralph warned. "He is quick and could take your eyes out. I suggest you go and talk to Growl about Vinnie. And speaking of Growl, I'd best go and update him on things," Ralph said as Rita nodded. He knew that Growl would certainly be unhappy to hear about the trouble Ditty had caused the night before. And with a nod to Pillow and Rita, Ralph headed off toward Growl's cave.

As Ralph approached Diggets Cave, he could see that Growl was lying outside of the cave. He looked very dirty, as if he had been sitting in the storm all night. He was also very still.

"Growl, why are you so muddy?" Ralph called out.

But Growl didn't move.

Ralph moved closer.

"No, oh no," Ralph howled with grief, and fell down next to Growl, tenderly pawing his master who had been like a father to him.

CHANGES ON THE ISLAND

Vinnie was waiting back at Willows Rock. He was spacing up and down, thinking how he was going to turn this situation around to his own advantage. He looked up and saw Pillow leading all the cats back to the colony. He had already heard the news about Growl and felt smug that finally the old boy would now be digging up weeds.

Pillow hurried over to Vinnie. "Are you okay? Where were you all night?"

"Why I stayed here, worried sick about everyone. I made sure no one was left behind. It was tough down here. I could barely keep my feet on the ground. I was swept from tree to tree like a flying monkey," Vinnie said. He saw Loops standing with Musette. "Even though you left your Catton, Loops, I made sure no one was left behind. And I thought we were a team, you and I," he added, trying to manipulate her as he had always done.

"You did no such thing, Vinnie," Loops said. "You stayed underground like one of the rats, probably getting drunk and falling asleep without even giving us a second thought. I'm tired, Vinnie." Loops flapped her paws to her sides. "I'm tired of you, and I'm tired of making excuses for you. I really need to think about us. I love you with my whole heart, Vinnie, but I don't like you."

"I will take that as a compliment," said Vinnie, knowing all eyes were on him and trying to be tough.

"Come along, Loops," said Musette. "He's not worth it. Let's get you home."

"That's *my* home!" shouted Vinnie, "Just so you don't forget! But you can stay there for now. I don't need you homeless as well as Cattonless," he blustered.

By now Danny, Vernon, and Spit had reached Vinnie. But they just ignored him and, without a single word, walked right by.

"Hey, boys!" Vinnie's tone was a bit desperate. "I think I've scared all of those vicious Doggeroes away, then, ehhhh? Who's left up there, a bunch of kittens I'm guessing…?"

"No," Pillow replied sternly. "Up there are decent, kind, and strong allies who saved our lives."

"Ha!" said Vinnie. "They knew if they hadn't taken in my, and I say *my* Cataquerians, I would have gone up there and taken those Doggeroes' eyes out."

But Pillow only shook his head. "I doubt that very much, Vinnie."

"You have no idea how much news travels, considering you harbor a gossip called Tibby who spreads news quicker than the twittering birds."

"What are you going on about now, Vinnie?" Pillow asked sternly.

"I actually spoke to Growl before you saw him. We had a meeting in secret, and I told him to look after my colony or else there would be trouble. I also told him to be nice to you, Pillow, since you're a wimp, and not to growl at you," Vinnie smirked.

The fur on Pillow's back went up higher than the mountains. He was angry like never before. "You're a *LIAR*, Vinnie. How *DARE* you mention the name of such a great leader who gave us all protection and who you clearly know is now gone. I am warning you, Vinnie, don't say another word." Pillow walked away, shaking with fury.

Vinnie sat there, astounded at Pillow's response, feeling as if he had been hit by a coconut. "So, Pillow has grown a backbone. Well, I'll snap it in two if he carries on with that attitude," Vinnie grumbled. But he sat there alone as everyone passed him by, like he wasn't even there.

In the aftermath of the hurricane, everything began to change in the colony. The kittens were learning to stay within a certain radius of the colony. The mums began going out more to hunt, while leaving their Cattons at home with the kittens. Tibby began to teach everyone how to record the days and weeks, and he was adding more information regarding events, school times, and general news to the colony's journal.

While everyone was getting on with the business of life, and enjoying it, Vinnie was becoming more and more bitter every day. He realized his opinions and ideas no longer seemed to count in the colony at all. He spent most of his time in his underground hut where he festered and plotted against everyone.

After the hurricane, Vinnie found a pair of binoculars on shore while wandering around and scrounging for items he could add to his collection in his den. When he found the binoculars, he put them to his eyes and looked through them just as Twinkles appeared before him.

"Good lord!" Vinnie screamed in fright and dropped them to the floor. He realized he'd been able to see Twinkles sitting on the beach with Tibby.

When Vinnie heard that Pillow, Musette, and Tibby were on the lookout for ships passing by the island, he decided to give the binoculars to Pillow. *If they can spot a ship through these things and finally leave my island, all the better!*

One day Vinnie found Pillow and gave him the binoculars. "Here, take these," he said flippantly. "Maybe they'll help get you off this island and do us all a favor. And take Twinkles with you," Vinnie sniggered.

"Why, thank you," Pillow said, genuinely surprised at Vinnie's offer. "These must have fallen off a ship and washed to shore." He held the binoculars and suddenly felt a yearning to return to civilization. "I will take theses to Tibby since he and Ditty are now watching out for ships."

"Ha! That annoying, scrappy little rat should go with you. He reminds me of Growl," muttered Vinnie.

Pillow ignored the comment and decided to try to be nice to Vinnie. "I guess you miss Loops. Your claws could do with a good sharpening," he chuckled.

"My claws are sharper than before! I have other means to get these beauties sharp," Vinnie grinned and held up a paw. "At least I don't get told what to do like you."

"It's not like that, Vinnie. I respect Musette. I know she can go on a bit but don't all Cattonas?" he said with a gentle laugh.

"Enough," said Vinnie, suddenly feeling rather sad. "I ain't listening to you, Pillow. Just go back to my Cataquerians and tell them I am too busy to deal with their dramas."

"Okay," Pillow said, and walked away, leaving Vinnie sitting alone, and secretly hoping Loops would come and get him. He hadn't been home since the storm. He had been certain Loops would beg him to come home, but she hadn't.

Danny, Spit, and Vernon spent more time with Pillow, who they respected. He had a different type of strength, and they trusted him. They had all learned that the island was a big place they could now explore.

One day Pillow, Musette, and Tibby were talking with them.

"Perhaps we could even meet other packs of dogs, too," Vernon suggested. "Before the storm, we never felt it was right to leave our territory. We have spent so much time living in fear of this and that. Even when we've seen ships passing by close to the island, all we've done is hide, thinking we would be killed by people just as we thought the Doggeroes would prey on us."

"People will never kill you unless you threaten them," Tibby said. "They are wise and mostly kind, so there is no need to worry about approaching them with caution. The main worry is that they might try to bring you aboard, believing they were saving you or doing you more good than harm."

"How often does a ship appear?" Pillow asked.

Spit thought for a few seconds. "I think the last time we saw one was when it was really hot, so I guess that was just before you three arrived on the island."

"That close?" Pillow asked Pillow excitedly.

"Yeah, I think they were fishing or something like that because they kept jumping into the ocean," Danny informed.

"Wow, that is amazing! We could be reunited with our wonderful owners one day, Musette!" Pillow exclaimed.

But Musette didn't feel quite as excited as Pillow at this possibility. She had truly settled into island life and had made many friends. She was even busy planning Suzy Wong's wedding to Mickey, who finally asked her to cross paws. Musette said, looking at Tibby, "Well, I do hope that's not until Tibby has found a mate. I would love to plan his wedding. He's so official and knowledgeable, any available Cattona would be proud to call him her Catton."

""Of course," Tibby puffed up at Musette's kind words. "Who else has my brains and looks?"

"Looks?" Danny chuckled. "Tibby, you may know a lot of things, but you ain't no looker, that's for sure!"

Everyone laughed, even Tibby. All the Cataquerians were so much happier since Vinnie had been leaving everyone alone.

At this moment, he was lying behind the huts, listening to the sounds of laughter.

I will get my revenge on them all one day, he thought. *One day, my day will come.*

THE SHIP

Days weeks and months passed on the island, and life flourished for the Cataquerians and the Doggeroes. At the colony, everyone was busy. Pillow had shown the Cataquerians how much easier life could be with a bit of carpentry. He taught them how to build storerooms for tools, beds, and small carts to carry large amounts of fish up from the beach. He was enjoying being busy and helping everyone work together to sets things right after the hurricane.

Ralph and Hans had been down to Willows Rock to sit and chat with the Cataquerians. They also hoped they might catch a glimpse of Vinnie who always seemed to conveniently be hiding in his underground den.

The kittens and puppies often played together, and even competed in small events organized by Musette and Loops, who both adored the puppies as much as the kittens.

Ditty spent as much time as he could at Willows Rock helping however he could. He loved Pillow so much, not only because he had saved Ditty's life, but also because he was so very tolerant and kind. Ditty loved to hear Pillow talk about living with Mr. and Mrs. Supreme and life in England. Ditty decided that one day he wanted to travel and see the world, too, just like Pillow had.

One morning, Ditty started yapping non-stop, breaking the lovely silence of the day.

Now what's wrong with him? thought Tibby, who was trying to sleep.

Ditty suddenly dashed right by Tibby, out of breath and hardly able to speak. "There's a ship, there's a ship!" he gasped. "It's big, with massive red sails! And I saw a little boat going over the side! I need to say good-bye to everyone! I'm going off to see the world!" And he raced out of the colony and up to Diggets Cave to tell Ralph and Rita.

Tibby sat up, picked up the binoculars Pillow had given him, and peered through them. He couldn't believe it! There was a big wooden ship offshore. He could just about make out the writing on its sails: *Hong Kong Star.* Tibby gasped. *Oh, my days,* he thought, *it must be heading to where our dear Supremes are. Finally, they were going to be rescued!* He raced through the colony, looking for Pillow and Musette. "Pillow! Musette! It's here! It's here! We're going home!"

Pillow rushed out of his hut. "Home? What are you talking about?"

"A ship, dear fellow, I'm talking about a ship approaching the shore!" Tibby informed.

"Oh, whiskers!" Pillow exclaimed. "I must tell Musette!" He was thrilled to the paws and just couldn't contain himself. "Musette! Musette!" he screamed.

"What on earth is going on?" she said, popping up outside their hut.

"It's a ship, darling! It's a ship!" Pillow exclaimed. "A ship's approaching shore! Why, we could be on it very soon and Tibby is certain it is heading to Hong Kong."

"Oh, I didn't think it would be this soon." Musette looked around. Kittens were playing, some counting pebbles, others being good and staying near their homes. Mums were grating coconuts for milk and others were marinating fish for Suzy and Mickey's upcoming wedding.

"What is it?" Pillow asked, noticing the look on Musette's

face and the hesitation in her voice.

"… nothing," she said. "It's just … I don't know what will happen if we leave. What if Vinnie brainwashes everyone again?"

"Oh, he's long gone," Pillow said. "Vinnie couldn't brainwash a stone these days. He's drunk all the time on fermented sugar cane."

"I know, but what about the kittens? And what about Loops? She is like a sister to me."

"What are you trying to say, Musette? You can tell me the truth," Pillow said gently. "I can only be happy if you are. What do you truly want?"

"I want to see our dear Supremes, I really do. I love and miss them so much. It's just that I've discovered a different kind of love, a more independent, natural way. I love being free and it just being the two of us, with you taking care of me and me taking care of you. I don't think I could go back to being fed and pampered and having little to do. I've changed, and I don't want to leave, Pillow. I feel this is our home now."

Pillow hugged Musette. "If staying here will make you happy, it will make me so as well. I'm very content here. I don't need fancy things anymore, or a bustling life in a big city."

"Well, I do, old boy," Tibby said, "I really do."

Pillow turned to Tibby. "All right, Tibby. I will help you get on board that ship if that is what you really want."

Tibby looked surprised. "Are you sure you're not coming?"

Pillow shook his head, "Yes, Tibby, we're staying. We can't leave our new friends. They have come to rely on us, and we are happy here on this beautiful island."

HUNTERS FOR FOOD

Ditty was telling Ralph and Rita all about his plans. "I am going get on the ship and sail to a place where people live like the Supremes and I will get fed and clothed and watch the television. Oh, I am so excited!"

Rita was crying. "But Ditty, we will miss you so much. Please don't go!"

"Don't cry, Mum! I am needed where people live. Tibby told me all about how I would make a great companion to Mrs. Supreme. I also want to see where my great ancestors came from," Ditty proudly announced. "And I will have a real purpose as Tibby says." Ditty was suddenly full of self-confidence and looked happy and lively.

"Now, now," Ralph told Rita gently, "he is not ours to keep, Rita. No Doggeroe is owned on this island, not even our dear Ditty. We must let him go, with love."

Ditty finally sat still for a moment, his head cocked to one side and his tail wagging with joy. Rita wrapped her paws around him and hugged him tight.

"Listen, my little one. You will always have a purpose and home on this island, don't you ever forget that, do you hear me?" And she squeezed him tighter than ever before.

"Yes!" Ditty said. "I won't!" and he ran off to dig a hole, for he was so excited that he couldn't keep still.

Musette decided to go and tell Loops that she wasn't leaving. News travelled fast on in the colony and she was worried Loops might be thinking all sorts.

"And I'd better go and speak with Rita and Ralph, too," Pillow told Musette. "They will be wondering what's going on. No doubt Ditty has rushed in guns blazing as he does, so I better head off and explain a few things."

As Pillow approached Diggets Cave, he could see Rita chatting to Ralph with tears streaming down her face.

Pillow walked straight to Rita. "I am sorry," he said, holding Rita's paw. "I hope you understand that I had to explain what life is like with humans to Ditty. He is such an inquisitive soul. I know it's hard to let Ditty go, but he really will have a wonderful life once he makes it to a new home. Hong Kong it a vibrant city with many people. Tibby will do his best to find our family, the Supremes. But wherever Ditty goes, he will be fed and loved by a family or even one person. He will have a good life as we once had with humans, I promise you. We just need to get him and Tibby onto the ship safely."

"And how do you intend to do that?" Ralph asked.

"All Tibby and Ditty need to do is get to the beach and wait there, looking as cute as possible. That's all it will take." Pillow chuckled. "As soon as the humans come to shore and spot Tibby and Ditty, they'll automatically take them in. It's what humans do. All Ditty needs to do is wag his tail while Tibby purrs. It's easy peasy. But they need to get down to the beach for the humans will be on shore very soon."

"I will come down with you," said Hans, trying to be strong.

But Pillow noticed how nervous Hans seemed. "Why don't you say goodbye here, Hans? We may not have time to do so once we get down on the shore. Plus, no offense, Hans, but you could possibly scare them away. You're a very big dog, the kind humans tend to approach with caution."

Hans nodded and approached Ditty. "Hey little brother," he said, "show them you're the boss over there, okay?"

"I will!" said Ditty excitedly.

Hans brushed Ditty's head with his pig paw. "Now, get out of here!"

"I'm ready!" Ditty exclaimed, and he hugged Rita and Ralph tightly.

"Don't worry," said Pillow, "Musette and I will hide in the bushes until you are picked up, okay, Ditty?" Ditty nodded. "Come on then, little one," Pillow said, and they both raced back down to Willows Rock.

Musette was crying her heart out and Pillow was trying to be brave as well, for neither really wanted Tibby to go. The other Cataquerians gathered to bid Tibby good-bye, but they were all relieved that Pillow and Musette had decided to stay.

"Come on, we have no time to waste. Let's go," Pillow said.

"I'll come with you, to say a proper goodbye," Musette told Tibby. And then they raced down to the shore.

When they reached it, Ditty was already waiting on the beach. They all saw one small rowboat making its way to shore. There were two men in it; one was sitting and rowing, and the other one had a telescope pointed toward the group on the beach.

"I think they have seen us," Pillow said.

"This is it, then." Musette hugged Tibby with all her might.

He was crying. "I can't stay, I'm sorry, but I just can't. I need my comforts," he said between the sobs.

"I know," Musette said gently. "It's okay, Tibby. But you must come back and see us."

"You bet I will," said Tibby. "Stay still now, Ditty."

"Okay, I will. Do I look cute? Ditty asked.

"You look adorable," Musette told him.

"We'll wait behind the trees until you have gone," Pillow told Tibby and Ditty. And with one backward glance at them,

Pillow and Musette moved toward the trees.

The men in the small boat were getting closer. They had tan skin, black hair, and narrow eyes. They were carrying rifles strapped over their shoulders and were chatting about what they could hunt once they had landed on shore.

"I think I will try and get a boar so we can have a nice stew," Chang said. He was a big stocky man with greasy black hair that flapped over his forehead like a flat handkerchief. His hands were rough and cracked and he rowed the small boat as if he was gliding through air.

The other man, Pong, smiled, showing his very black teeth. "I will shoot anything that moves. I am that hungry."

"As long as it's not me," said Chang laughing.

As the boat got closer to the beach, Tibby and Ditty could hear the men talking, but they didn't understand a word they were saying for they spoke very fast. Finally, Pong, who was very tall and muscular, jumped out of the boat and, splashing through the low tide, started to drag it to the shore.

"Ah," he said, when he saw Tibby and Ditty, who was now waving his tail with excitement. "Look what we have here," he said to Chang while pointing at Tibby and Ditty.

"Very good," said Chang, who had waded through the water. "You have saved me bullets," he said and grabbed Ditty with one hand. He held him up by his throat as Ditty's eyes bulged. "Yes, nice and tasty!"

Tibby gasped. *Oh no, these humans are hunting for food!* He jumped into the air, trying to get to Ditty, but was shoved to the ground by the man who shouted, "You, too, Gloves!"

Gloves? Tibby thought, confused. But then he realized what the man meant, for he was staring at Tibby's soft fur and nodding.

Pillow and Musette had seen everything. "Run! Run for

your life!" Pillow hissed to Musette, and when she ran off, Pillow rushed out from the cover of the trees onto the sand and flung himself at the man, scratching and clawing at his face, trying to get him to drop Ditty.

Suddenly Pillow felt himself grabbed so roughly by the scruff of the neck he could hardly breath.

"You want to fight, huh?" growled the man. "I will put you in a stew and see how you like that!"

Chang ordered Pong to go and fetch the sack from the boat. He kept his foot firmly on Ditty who was wiggling like a snake in the sand. "Hurry," he told Pong, "I want to take them back alive, so they stay fresh."

Pong splashed through the water as quick as he could and grabbed the sack. He rushed it back to Chang who opened it and shoved in Ditty followed by Pillow, and then Tibby.

Ditty was crying and yelping. "I don't like people! I've changed my mind! I want to go home!"

"That was easy," Pong said. "Let's get back to the ship and have a nice fresh lunch." And he laughed.

Musette had run as fast as she could back to Willows Rock. Although she could hardly breathe, she somehow managed to scream, "Help! Help! Someone, please help!"

Danny came running up to her. "What's up, sweet cakes? Calm down."

But Musette couldn't for she was frantic. "It's Tibby and Ditty! They've been snatched by Chinese hunters who are going to eat them! I heard it! And I think they've got Pillow now, too!" She was crying uncontrollably.

Loops was now by her side, gasping, "Oh no, no!" She held her paws to her small face.   Vinnie came strolling up, looking calm and smug. "Well, well, well, so Pillow has finally left our shores," he smirked.

Loops ran up to Vinnie. "Help, Vinnie, I'm begging you! We need you do something!"

He looked at her. "Do something? Haven't I done enough by giving Pillow my binoculars? I finally got something right!" And he laughed.

Musette turned to him, hissing, "You vile, horrible creature, how could you find this funny?"

"Now, now, settle, Petal. I'll bring him back, don't you worry about that," Vinnie said, thinking, *This is my chance to gain back my power.*

Loops stared at him, hoping he sincerely meant it. She flung her paws around him in desperation and hugged him. Vinnie froze. He hated public displays of affection. "Enough of that, move away, my little ray of sunshine."

Vernon and Spit had joined the group and stood next to Danny. "What's the plan then? We don't have time to waste," Spit said.

"How are we going to get to the ship? We can't swim that far," Vernon added.

"We could ask Ralph," Musette said. "He could swim us out there."

"'Us'? You ain't going nowhere, young lady," said Spit.

"Musette and I will go to Diggets Cave to speak with Ralph," said Loops. "Come on, Musette, there's no time to waste."

They hurried off as Vinnie sat with the others, waiting and thinking. He imagined Pillow being stirred in a pot. Vinnie hadn't felt this happy in a long time.

Inside the sack, the cats and pup could hear the men chatting as they rowed back to the ship. Ditty was terrified while Pillow tried to get his wits about him.

"Don't worry," said Tibby. "It will be fine."

"I know," Pillow answered bravely. "We will work it out."

"Will we?" Ditty asked. "I am so scared. I just want to go home."

"You mustn't fret, Ditty," Pillow reassured him. "Help will come. I just know it."

They could feel the waves beneath the boat, rocking it side to side as the men rowed. Tibby, Ditty, and Pillow sat silently, waiting to be taken from out of the darkness.

Musette and Loops finally reached Diggets Cave. They were both panting frantically for they hadn't stopped once in their run from the colony. All the dogs began yapping and barking, their tails wagging in excitement upon seeing the two Cataquerians.

"Hello," said Ralph, appearing outside the cave. "What brings you two young ladies up here? Rita, come and say hi to the girls," he shouted out.

"It's Pillow and Tibby!" Musette gasped. Her throat hurt because it was so dry.

"Goodness, calm down, Musette," said Rita who had joined Ralph. "Just take a deep breath and then tell us what has happened."

"Tibby and Ditty were waiting on the beach. And these hunters came off the boat. They grabbed them, held them by their throats, and talked about how they were going to eat them once they got them onto their ship. Pillow ran out to help, but I'm sure he was no match for those men!"

"Oh no!" Rita collapsed in shock and grief. "My Ditty, my Ditty," she sobbed.

"Where is the boat now," Ralph asked.

"It's just offshore," said Loops.

"Can it be seen from the beach?" Ralph asked.

"Yes," said Musette. "It's not that far out. We need to get to it. Ralph, can you swim us out to it?"

In reply Ralph shouted for Hans, Loco, and Stone, who were the strongest swimmers on the island. Then he turned back to the girls. "You stay here together. I promise we will bring everyone back safely. But you stay here and try to keep calm."

Hans, Loco, and Stone rushed up. Loco was a grey dog with a wiry coat that stuck up in the air like it was permanently electrified. He had narrow eyes and spent much time sleeping. However, he loved the water and could fish for hours on the shore, swimming in and out of the water, searching for the biggest catch of the day. Often, he caught so many fish that he'd drop many of them back into the ocean so they could swim away.

Stone was a large, longhaired dog. His fur was brown and white, and as soft as a warm duvet. He had big muscles. He, too, didn't do much other than sleep most days or swim in the sea. Stone had a good heart and was kind and loveable. He had made good friends with most of the Cataquerians and was shocked and saddened to hear of their troubles.

"Come on, we have no time to waste!" said Ralph. "We must be quick before the ship sets sail away from the island."

"That's if they haven't already," said Stone.

"Let's go!" Hans cried, and led the way down from Diggets Cave.

All four of them raced down into Willows Rock. When Vinnie saw them, he grinned. "Well, well, well, what do we have here?" he asked in his usual twisted tone.

"You know who I am," Ralph said.

Hans was rigid, his tail was straight, and along his back, a line of fur stood up. "I could bite your head off right now if I wanted to, but there's enough drama going on as it is without you adding to it!" he told Vinnie.

"Now, now, less of that attitude," Vinnie said. "I was actually going to help rescue them, but since you're being like this, you lot can get to that boat and take your chances."

"We could do with your help, Vinnie," Ralph said. "I mean look at those amazing claws of yours. They'd terrify anyone, even humans."

"If you jump on my back," Stone added, "I will swim out with you. I promise you that you will be safe."

"Jump on your back? You must be joking. I wouldn't trust a Doggeroe with my life." Vinnie said.

"I didn't think you meant it when you said you wanted to rescue them," Ralph sneered. "You're nothing more than a coward, Vinnie."

Furious, Vinnie arched his back, flipped out his claws, and screamed, "Me a coward, standing here up against you bunch of long-legged wimps?!"

"Well, come on then," said Ralph cunningly. "Jump on Stone's back if you're not afraid." Ralph knew they needed Vinnie who could take out the eyes of the hunters. And Ralph's words worked on Vinnie, who didn't want to be seen as a coward.

"Okay," Vinnie said, and leapt onto Stone's back like a black, poisonous frog. *I'll come*, he thought, *but I won't be bringing that wishy-washy Pillow back to my island.*

Danny, who was close by, said, "Hold steady, I'm coming, too," and jumped onto Loco's back.

And they all rushed to the shore.

Once there, they could see the large wooden boat was

about a mile out in the ocean. They didn't know exactly what they'd do when they reached it, but they weren't going to give up without putting up a fight for Pillow, Tibby, and Ditty.

In his mind, Ralph could still see Pillow risking his own life to save Ditty during the hurricane. Now, with his whole heart, Ralph wanted to save Pillow.

Ralph turned to Stone. "You swim out first, and Loco, Hans, and I will follow behind you."

Stone nodded and, with Vinnie on his back, walked into the water and began to swim, as Loco, Hans, and Ralph followed. The water was warm, and the current was mild as they effortlessly floated and drifted along with the waves.

Vinnie, latched onto Stone, was not really enjoying the sensation of being beholden to a Doggeroe. Most of the cats on Cataquerians Island could swim, but not as far as these dogs could.

Danny was chatting away to Loco about how happy he was that everyone was finally getting along, and even Vinnie was now part of this new way of living together in harmony.

Vinnie rolled his eyes in utter disbelief. "What is wrong with you?" he asked Danny. "Would you stop yakking and just get on with it. I must be mad," he muttered, gritting his teeth, "going to rescue that annoying Catton. I hope he gets stuck in the hunters' throats. It'd save us the bother of killing them."

"Killing?" Hans asked. "We are not killing anyone, not even the hunters."

"Well, let's not go in shaking hands, either," said Ralph. "We need to be aware that these humans consider us prey, so just be careful, Hans."

"As for that Tibby, he's probably sinking the boat anyway," added Vinnie.

SACK OF CATS

As the rowboat reached the dark wooden ship, Chang called out, "We're back!" When he stood up, the boat rocked side to side.

A young boy named Hop appeared at the ship's rail above the rowboat. He was brown, tall, and willowy with curly dark hair and hardly had any teeth.

"Catch!" yelled Chang. And he threw a long rope up to Hop, who caught it effortlessly and tied the rope securely to the side of the ship. "Give me the sack, Pong," Chang ordered. When he had it in hand, he threw it high into the air, right onto the big ship's wooden deck.

"Ouch!" Ditty yelled.

"Ooooof," Tibby muttered as Pillow rolled into him. "I'm too old for this."

"Sorry, Tibby," Pillow said. "But we need to listen to what's going on."

Pong and Chan then climbed a swaying rope ladder up to the big ship. Once on board, they instructed Hop to take the sack to the galley for lunch.

"That's nice," said Ditty. "At least we will get something to eat."

"Yes, we will," Tibby said, not wanting to scare him. But Tibby and Pillow shared a look, for they knew what that "something to eat" was going to be.

They could hear the ship's wooden deck creaking as Hop walked along it briskly, whistling away.

In the galley, Hop placed the big sack on a table. "Don't worry, furry food," he said, "I will make it as quick and painless as possible for you, with just a quick slit to the throat." He opened the sack and first took out Pillow. "I don't like you. You won't go with my coat. So, it's stew for you." He put Pillow in a cage in the corner. The cage already held a big rat that was cowering and shaking.

"Hello, I'm Pillow. I take it you're the starter then?"

"No, I'm supposed to be lucky because apparently, it's the Year of the Rat. I'm Pip."

"Oh," said Pillow. "It's not the year of the cat, that's for sure."

The rat gulped. "Could my day get any worse? I do hope you're not intending to have me as your last meal!"

"Oh, don't worry," said Pillow, smiling bravely. "We're going to get out of here, and you, too."

Hop then pulled Tibby out of the sack. "I like you, but I've already got a coat in your color. There's plenty of meat on you, though." And Hop tossed Tibby into the cage with Pillow and Pip.

Next, Hop pulled Ditty from the sack. "Ahhhh, much better, nice color. And perfect for some new gloves. You can stay here," he said, grabbing a rope and tying Ditty to a hook hanging from the galley ceiling. But Ditty's little legs could barely touch the ground, and the rope was so tight he could barely breathe. He whined weakly, which made Hop laugh. "Whine away, little dog, because you will be giving high fives after lunch once I'm wearing you on my hand!"

By now Tibby could hardly breathe because he was so scared. "What are we going to do?" he moaned as he watched in horror at Ditty pulling and tugging at the long rope.

"Stop moving, Ditty!" Pillow shouted. "You're going to hurt yourself. Just try to stay calm."

DOGGEROES ON THE SHIP

As the four dogs swam closer and closer to the ship, they began to feel anxious but also excited. Knowing they would soon face the enemy, they suddenly felt a powerful, strong, and fearless force had entered their bodies.

They could see the rope ladder hanging down over the side of the big ship.

"Listen, Vinnie," said Ralph, "you go up first with Danny, and then Hans and I will follow. Stone and Loco, you stay in the water and wait. You can hold onto the ladder once we're up top. And save your strength since we may need to swim back to shore fast!"

Vinnie was up the rope like a rat up a drainpipe, with Danny close behind him.

"Listen," Danny whispered. They could hear two men chatting away and laughing.

"I hope Hop has that stew going by now. I am so hungry," said one voice.

"Yeah, and that big one looks like he will feed us for a week," laughed the other.

Vinnie sniggered. "You're not wrong there."

Danny shook his head at Vinnie. "Come on. We need to be quick."

"That's if they're still alive," said Vinnie smugly.

Once on the deck, Vinnie and Danny looked around. The ship was long and narrow. Plenty of nets, ropes, and harpoons were lying around on the deck. Black and slippery, it creaked as if it was going to snap into bits at any moment. And everything smelled fishy and dirty.

Danny spotted some steps leading down to a dark door. "Come on," he told Vinnie, "they must be down there."

They slowly crept down the stairs. Through the gap of some swinging wooden doors, they could see Ditty dangling from that rope, his paws barely touching the ground.

"Oh my, what a sight! I can't remember when I had so much fun," Vinnie chuckled.

Danny turned around and snarled at Vinnie for the first time ever. "You fool, he is going to choke to death if we don't do something fast."

Vinnie was speechless. Danny had never spoken to him that way before. Vinnie also knew that Danny was his match. So he tried to lighten the mood. "Can't even make a joke these days?"

"Nothing about this is funny!" Danny hissed. "Come on, let's get to it!" Danny suddenly flung himself at the wooden doors. They flew open like a newspaper blowing in the wind, and within seconds Vinnie leapt into the air with one clean swipe, slicing through the rope in seconds with his razor-like claws. Freed, Ditty fell to the floor and began running around in circles, yapping and gasping for air.

"Oh shut up!" hissed Vinnie.

"Look! It's Danny!" said Tibby.

"Are we pleased to see you!" Pillow added.

Danny hurried over to the cage. He began pushing the long metal pole with his paw, trying to slide it across when all of a sudden Hop grabbed him by the back of his neck.

"Where did you come from?" Hop asked. Suddenly, he felt an enormous sharp pain in his ankle. Ditty was hanging onto it with his sharp, needle-like teeth.

"AAAGGHHHH!" Hop screamed. "You rotten little beast. I'll hook you up by your throat!" He leaned down to grab Ditty.

Vinnie leapt onto Hop's head and dug every one of his claws so deep into his scalp that his hair began to fall onto the floor in clumps.

Danny ran to the cage and with one almighty push, slid the bolt across so the door opened.

Ditty was now on the top on the galley worktop. Hop had taken a big cleaver and was about to take his head off when Ralph jumped onto Hop and knocked him to the floor. Growling, he bared his huge teeth right into Hop's face and the boy shook with fear.

"Run for it!" Ralph barked at the others as he held Hop in place.

Hans was by his side now, growling and barking loudly.

"Go, go!" shouted Ralph.

"No way," said Hans. "I'm staying here until we are all off of this decrepit old floating tree."

On the deck, Chan and Pong stopped mending nets when they saw Ditty, Pillow, and Tibby running to side of the ship with two other cats. On top of that, Pip was running along with them.

"What was that?!" shouted Chan.

"It's a banquet, that's what!" Pong yelled, rolling his sleeves up as if he was going into battle.

Both men ran down to the galley only to find Hop quivering on the floor as Hans and Ralph stood over him.

"Ah, so now we have something to put on the spit," said Chang staring at the two dogs. Ralph glanced at Hans. They knew they were in trouble for both men were big and appeared to have no fear. They were hunters and had faced many wild dogs on their travels.

189

"I will get the wiry one," Chan said. "You take the white one. Let's do this."

Hans started to bark so loudly that the ship rocked with the vibration. Hans made eye contact with Pong, who suddenly understood he had met his match. "Come on then," he said as Hans felt excitement rushing through him. He could smell the fear suddenly coming from both men and he couldn't wait to sink his teeth deep into Pong. Hans's mouth was opened as wide as a hungry shark's, baring his big, white, very sharp teeth. He kept his eye on Pong until both men rushed toward the Doggeroes, going for their throats. Suddenly, Pip came running back into the room.

"Ahhhhhh!" screamed Chan. "It's the rat, the rat! Keep it away from me!" And he leapt onto the wooden worktop, screaming like a girl.

Pong tried to grab Hans while Hop tried to grab Pip, but Pip was fast and ran everywhere like a little piece of lightning. Hans growled and ran around behind Pong, chomped onto the back of his trousers, and shaking Pong violently as if he were a toy.

"Let go, you monster!" Pong screamed, while trying to wallop Hans on the head with his fist.

Hans released him when Vinnie, Danny, Pillow, and Tibby, who had raced back to the galley, scratched, bit and spit at Chan who was trying to fight them off.

"Oh, for heaven's sake, who is the rat?" Vinnie screeched, trying to swipe Pip with his claw.

"Leave the rat alone!" shouted Pillow. "He's with us!"

What next? Vinnie thought. *I can't cope.*

"Ahhhh, get away from me!" Chang screamed again. He was now crouching in the big galley sink, pathetically terrified that Pip would come near him. "You'll pay for this, Hop. You'll never work on this ship again!" Chan cried.

"I don't want to!" Hop shouted back. "I'm a vegetarian anyway. I've always known animals feel fear and pain. Run! All of you, run, go, go!" he cried.

Pong was sitting on the floor with his hands to his face. "Please get away from me. Just leave me and take that rat with you!"

"Come on," Pillow told Pip. "What are you waiting for? This is your lucky day."

Pip was looking dizzy and swaying. "Oh, I feel sick," he groaned.

"It's sea sickness!" shouted Tibby, poking his head out of the cage.

"I will carry you." And Pillow picked up Pip gently in his mouth.

"Now I've seen it all," Vinnie muttered.

Hans and Ralph started to back out of the room slowly. "I'll take Tibby," Ralph said, and grabbed Tibby in his mouth. Then he and Hans bolted from the room, with Tibby looking like a sack of potatoes hanging out of Ralph's mouth.

"This is brilliant," said Vinnie, loving the sight of Tibby being carted off in Ralph's mouth as he and Hans headed upstairs to the deck.

Danny, Pillow, and Vinnie all leapt onto the swinging doors at once so they could keep an eye on Hop, Chang, and Pong who were staring up at the three cats.

"Go, you two," Vinnie said. "I'll be the last to leave. We don't know when those three prawns may want a second round."

"Fine," said Danny, and he steadied himself and readied to jump onto the steps below. After he did, Vinnie motioned for Pillow to follow and, holding, Pip he did.

Vinnie then arched his back, hissing loudly, his claws out

as he took one last look at the three men. "You're pathetic, keeping a rat!" he hissed and flew into the air, swiping it with one of his claws, leaving the men on the floor dumbfounded.

All three cats were now on deck. They couldn't believe they had taken on man and won. This was a day they would never forget.

"We don't have any time to waste," Hans yelled, as he and Ralph joined the group. "Let's get off of this ship!"

Pip was standing there watching them all go overboard. "Well, 'bye then," he said sadly.   "Come on!" said Pillow. "Jump down onto my back."

"Oh, this is becoming comical," Vinnie said, looking at Pip. "I mean I can't ignore him, I just can't. I'm getting hungry."

"Yes, you can," Pillow said. "He is a lucky rat and it's the Year of the Rat. And if he is harmed, I don't know what would lay in store for you, Vinnie."

"Oh, that's all mumbo jumbo, but I won't touch him. I've had enough drama for one day." But then Vinnie thought to himself, *I'll get him once we're on shore.*

As they all clambered over the ladder, they felt tired but elated from the fight.

Stone and Loco were so happy to see them all.

"You made it then. Thank goodness for that," Stone said.

And as everyone headed for shore, swimming through the calm waters, evening was drawing in and the darkening sky seemed like a giant, warm blanket floating toward Cataqueria Island.

41

RETURNING HOME

As the dogs paddled toward the shore of Cataqueria Island, with their passengers on their backs, everyone was silent, for all understood that they were all one from now on.

Musette, Rita, and Suzy Wong were on the beach, waiting, praying, and hoping that everyone would return from the ship safely. Twinkles came down with a large bowl of coco milk and sat by the girls. Suddenly Musette shouted, *"LOOK! LOOK! IT'S THEM! THEY'RE COMING! LOOK!"* The girls could see the dark silhouettes on the waves, softly bouncing towards them like bubbles floating in the air.

Ditty jumped off Ralph's back first, splashing into the water and paddling toward the beach. When he could stand on the sand, he shouted, "Mum! Mum!" and ran straight to Rita, jumping up at her face and yelping, this time with glee.

"Oh Ditty, she sighed, "Ditty, you're home."

Hans ran over to Rita, too. She touched his paw and held it tightly for a few seconds. Then he gently pulled his paw away and smiled at her with love.

Soon everyone had reached shore. Ralph was exhausted, and collapsed onto the sand, with Hans, Stone, and Loco nearby.

Pillow was in Musette's arms, and she was crying.

Tibby was greeted by Twinkles. "I hope you didn't come here just for me," he said.

"I thought you might need someone to talk to, Tibby. It

must have been a shock to have your hopes shattered."

"It was, Twinkles, but it was even worse to think I was going to be some human's supper!"

"Come on, then, let's get you a drink," Twinkles said, and Tibby gratefully let her lead him to the milk.

Vinnie made his way back to his hut in silence. He had decided to go home just to test the waters with Loops. When he entered the hut, she looked up and smiled, so very glad he was safe.

"Ahhh, stop grinning. I'm just here to sleep," Vinnie told her.

"I am so proud of you for helping to rescue our friends," Loops said.

"Friends?" said Vinnie, but he calmed himself. "I still wouldn't trust that Pillow. Do you know he brought a rat back with us, not to eat but to rescue?" He slapped his head with a paw. "I mean what next? He'll soon be throwing the fish back into the sea."

Loops started laughing, "Oh Vinnie, I'm so glad you're home."

Vinnie finally smiled. "Come here, my little sunbeam." He hugged Loops gently and her heart pounded like the great waves hitting the ocean. He then walked over to the shelf where his flint and coco butter were kept. He picked up the flint and walked towards Loops as her heart sank in dismay. But then, to her surprise, Vinnie walked past her and out through the front door. Loops followed.

Outside, she watched as Vinnie threw the flint as far as he could. Then he turned to her. "No more of that." And Loops ran into Vinnie's arms.

Back on the beach, Tibby and Twinkles sat alone with Pip. By now Pillow and Musette had headed straight to the colony to tell everyone what had happened, and the Doggeroes had headed back to Diggets Cave where their families waited.

Tibby looked at Pip. "Well, Pip, there are plenty of rats up by the fruit trees. Tomorrow I will take you there. Until then you are welcome to come back to our colony with me for the night."

And Pip said, "Thank you. I will. That's very kind of you," as Twinkles smiled at Tibby.

When Ralph, Rita, Hans, and Ditty reached Diggets Cave, they found all the other Doggeroes waiting for them, tails wagging and barking. Ditty was glad to see the pack and all the happy faces surrounding him. He suddenly knew that he belonged here. And he also realized that being in the pack meant something more than just digging holes and chasing vermin.

One of the excited puppies kept trying to jump onto Ditty's back but kept falling onto the floor. Ditty turned and barked once, deeply. "Don't be so rough," he told the pup. "I now need to go up and keep watch."

The other Doggeroes fell silent as Ditty walked slowly, looking very self-assured. His ears were up and his tail was still.

Ralph looked over to where he had found Growl after the storm and shivers ran down his spine. For a second, Ralph felt Growl's presence. Hans, who was standing next to Ralph, watched his little brother, feeling so very proud. And Rita smiled, silently saying goodbye to the puppy and hello to Ditty, The Doggeroe!!

THE WEDDING

Suzy Wong and Mickey were getting married in two days, so the island was buzzing. The Cataquerians and the Doggeroes were all working together to make this day a very special one. Musette was teaching everyone songs, which could be sung at the wedding, while Twinkles was busy rehearsing her solo piece. Even the Doggeroes were learning to sing.

The Doggeroes had decided to hunt for a large boar so everyone could feast. This would be a real treat for the Cataquerians, as they relied mainly on birds and rodents for meat.

Pip was now living with the fruit rats and was very happy. He, too, was looking forward to the wedding. Suzy Wong had told him that he could bring a plus one, but he couldn't find anyone who wanted to go. The other rats feared they might not be as lucky as Pip and could very easily end up in the stomach of a Cataquerian or a Doggeroe. They all treated Pip rather like royalty since none of the cats or dogs would touch him. Pip considered himself very lucky indeed.

Ralph and Pillow were sitting down at Willows Circle just chatting about how life was so very different.

"Can you imagine if you had never of jumped off that ship bound for Hong Kong all those months ago?" Ralph asked.

Pillow nodded. "Right. And now a hurricane has brought us all together."

"What about Vinnie, can you trust him yet?" Ralph asked.

"Well, I think Vinnie's a changed Catton," Pillow said. "And he did help rescue us, so I will never forget that."

"Did you hear that Ditty saw a ship yesterday?" Ralph asked.

"Yes, I did, and I bet he didn't race down to the beach this time," laughed Pillow.

"No, he didn't. He just stayed still waiting for it to pass. He is a great Doggeroe," said Ralph proudly. "He hardly leaves Diggets Cave these days. I swear, Pillow, he is turning into Growl."

"So, I've heard," said Pillow nodding his head in agreement. "Rita was telling Musette just the other day how much he has grown up."

And they both sat there, chatting away.

Vinnie and Loops were strolling around Willows Rock. He wasn't particularly looking forward to the wedding for he disliked all that romantic nonsense, but Loops said, "I can't wait to see Mickey and Suzy Wong cross paws. It will be so lovely."

"What's so lovely about it? Mickey will just get more of an earache from her," Vinnie grumbled.

Loops smiled and took Vinnie by the paw. "I've something to tell you, dear," she said smiling.

"What? I washed up the bowls. What do you want me to do next? Juggle with them?"

"No, just listen. I'm having kittens," Loops said.

"Oh, biting crabs," Vinnie said, for he wasn't really listening. Loops waited patiently. Suddenly Vinnie stopped. "What did you say?" He took Loops by the shoulders.

"I'm having kittens," she repeated.

"What?!" Vinnie started jumping up and down. "Oh my!" and he ran off yelling, "I'm going to be a dad! I'm going to be a dad!" leaving Loops there, smiling.

Spit, Mick, Vernon, and Danny were lying down on the ground outside of Danny's hut when Vinnie came running up.

"Did you hear me! I'm going to be a dad!" Vinnie crowed.

Spit laughed. "Oh yeah, Vinnie, we heard you all right!"

"Yup, I've still got it!" Vinnie grinned as his friends laughed with him, sharing his excitement.

By now all the Cataquerians began to gather to congratulate Vinnie given the commotion he was making.

Tibby said, "Congratulations, Vinnie," and then turned to Twinkles. "Little Vinnies! Heaven help us!" he whispered, which made Twinkles laugh.

And when Pillow and Ralph appeared and heard the news, Pillow told Vinnie, "That's fantastic news, Vinnie. I couldn't be happier for you."

And as everyone watched, Pillow held his paw out to Vinnie, who took it and crossed paws. In that moment, Pillow and Vinnie knew that they were united against anyone or anything that happened from that day onwards.

Then Ralph held out his paw, and Vinnie said, "Oh, what the heck?" and crossed paws with Ralph.

Meanwhile, Loops paid a visit to Musette who was in her hut, busy making pretty plated tiaras for Suzy Wong's big day. Musette looked up and smiled at her friend. "Well?" she asked Loops.

"I told him," she said, smiling brightly.

"What did he say?"

"He went crazy with joy! He told the entire colony! I know he'll be a wonderful father!"

I wouldn't go that far, thought Musette but she wouldn't spoil her friend's moment. "I'm sure he'll do just fine," she said and then found herself ready to cry.

"Oh, Musette," Loops said. "I know Pillow would have been a great dad, too."

Musette sniffled. "Sorry, I'm just being silly. It must be the wedding."

"Yes, weddings can be very emotional," Loops said, but she knew in her heart that Musette longed to be a mother.

That evening Vinnie was slicing up a coconut for his and Loops's supper when she said, "Vinnie, I need you to help me with something."

"Yes, sugar lump, anything," Vinnie replied, still feeling chuffed.

"Would you get the basket? We have work to do," she said. And Vinnie picked it up, thinking, *She probably has a craving for more coconuts*. And off they went together, holding paws.

The next day quite early, Pillow woke up to a sound. "What's that?" he said, and nudged Musette. "Do you hear that, Musette? Someone's kitten must have got lost and found its way in here."

They both heard the crying and screeching of a baby.

Musette quickly got up and rushed to the front door of the hut. There sat a basket. She opened it up to find four small kittens inside; three were fast asleep and one jet black one was standing with its paws gripping to the basket's sides, staring up at Musette and crying.

"Oh, my!" Musette cried, falling to her knees, bursting with love as Pillow appeared next to her. "Oh look, Pillow, at these precious angels!"

Loops and Vinnie suddenly appeared from the side of the hut.

"Welcome to my world," said Vinnie to Pillow. "Loops will explain. It was all her idea."

Loops moved to Musette's side. "Vinnie and I went out

yesterday evening to visit all the mums that had big litters. And we asked who would volunteer a baby for a wonderful mother and father. No one hesitated," said Loops, glowing with love.

"And don't forget that I stopped it at four," Vinnie said, "otherwise you would have ended up with a whole colony of kittens!"

Pillow started laughing. "Thanks, Vinnie. Four is plenty!"

"That's what I thought," Vinnie said.

Musette flung her arms around Loops, crying, "Thank you, Musette, thank you so much!" And then both Cattonas turned their attention back to the kittens.

"Best leave them to it," said Vinnie. "Do you fancy a stroll?"

"Yes, I do," said Pillow, as the other kittens began to wake up and the mewing grew louder.

As Vinnie turned to go, Musette said, "Vinnie?"

"Yes, firecracker, what?" he asked.

"Thank you," Musette said.

"Ahhh," he said, waving his paw at her, but he looked quite pleased.

It was the day of the wedding and the girls were getting bride Suzy Wong ready for her big day. Suzy Wing was trying to place the tiara on her sister's head. "Keep still, for heaven's sake," she said, but her twin was so excited, she couldn't be still.

"Give it here," said Musette. "Relax, Suzy. I can't put this on a bee that's buzzing." And Musette managed to secure the tiara in place by wrapping some small vines around Suzy's ears.

Suzy Wong looked beautiful and her eyes were sparkling like the glistening ocean.

All the Cattons were at Willows Circle putting up flowers around the huts while the Cattonas were laying out food on the long wooden table the Cataquerians had built. Rita placed in the table's center the large boar that had been slowly roasted and stood back feeling proud of her presentation. "Perfect!" she said.

Tibby was writing out a speech for Danny. "Please, keep it short and sweet, Tibby."

"I will," smiled Tibby.

Soon everyone began to arrive for the wedding, looking their best. The Doggeroes looked clean and bright, their tails were wagging, and they enjoyed the tasty snacks of roasted mice.

Finally, it was time for the ceremony. Pip called everyone to the ledge. He was standing in its center, on a tree trunk.

"Will the bride and groom come and stand up here," he said.

Mickey and Suzy Wong leapt onto the ledge.

Vinnie and Loops were holding hands. Vinnie, who was watching Pip, licked his lips as Loops watched him. She whispered, "Vinnie, stop that!"

"I can't help it, Loops," he whispered back. "I'm a Catton and he's a, well, you know…"

"Shhhhh," Loops hushed Vinnie, but she couldn't help but smile.

Musette and Pillow were next to Vinnie and Loops, holding their kittens under their paws. Vinnie motioned to Mickey and whispered to Pillow, "Poor chap, he doesn't know what he's in for, eh?"

Mickey was standing on the ledge and indeed looking very nervous. Pillow chuckled.

Tibby and Twinkles were standing next to each other. Tibby

took her paw and Twinkles knew she would be the next bride.

Pip asked for everyone to be quite but, given the chatting going on, no one could really hear him because he was so small. Vinnie noticed and took this opportunity to raise his voice. "Quiet everyone! Let's get this over and done with so we can eat and drink!" He smiled, and thought, *That felt good. It's been a while since I had a good shout.*

"Here, here!" Danny added, smiling. Sometimes he did miss the old Vinnie.

The ceremony went ahead and then the party began.

Pillow and Musette were sitting together, cuddling their kittens, enjoying the festivities, and remembering their very first days on Cataqueria Island when Tibby joined them.

"Did I see you holding paws with Twinkles?" teased Musette.

"You did indeed, young lady," said Tibby.

"Life is very different here on Cataqueria Island than when we first arrived," Pillow noted.

"Indeed it is, wonderfully so," said Tibby, looking at Twinkles who was singing.

Suddenly a huge flock of birds came flying over and began dropping petals down onto everyone, as if it was raining flowers.

It was Breeze and her flock, which began to squawk happily at the event below.

Pillow, Musette, and Tibby looked up, smiled and waved. They all felt truly blessed.

But Vinnie, being Vinnie, thought, *Oh lord, not more visitors!* He flicked the petals away from his face, and yelled, "Meeting!" as Pillow, Musette, Tibby, and Loops all began to laugh.

Born in London, Tabatha Taylor wanted to write from a young age. Moving to southern Spain in her thirties, raising three sons, and rescuing animals in the lovely, warm, rural countryside of Andalusia, inspired her to write *Cataqueria Island*, her first children's novel. Tabatha is a successful artist, but her passion for writing keeps knocking at the door.

www.ingramcontent.com/pod-product-compliance
Lightning Source LLC
Chambersburg PA
CBHW032129170626
46808CB00006B/2167

* 9 7 8 1 7 8 2 2 2 7 5 7 1 *